THE
Babymama
THE *Wife,*
& THE
Mistress

Tales of Women Scorned
2

A NOVEL BY

CANDY MOORE

CHAPTER ONE

Dornell

Freedom Soon Come

*T*his mothafucking prison is giving a nigga a mothafucking rash! Swear I'm getting hives and shit in this bitch. I sat in the yard on top of a long wooden table that was bolted to the ground, as I took in a game of basketball from the other inmates. Just watch, before y'all reach the end of this chapter this game is about to turn into a full fist fight. Somebody may even get stabbed...just wait for it.

I sat kicking it with the two ex-cons I have grown to get along with, Cedric and Steve. They both were in for armed robbery with a dangerous weapon and each got twelve years. Man! I don't know what I'd do if I had to spend a whole twelve years in the joint. Barely been in this shit hole three months, and I already feel as if I'm losing my goddamn mind.

So let me give the real story of how the fuck I done ended up in here. As you all already know, I took the rap for my girl, that materialistic bitch; but don't get me wrong, I mean the word bitch in a good way. Dedra was the type of female that just was never satisfied. I worked hard, put food on the table, and provided for her and the kids, making sure they never wanted for nothing. Sure, she couldn't rock designer shit like I know she wanted to, but she was living comfortable. But like a true female, that shit just wasn't enough.

So what does she do? She goes out, hooks up with one of the local dope boys who sells drugs on our block, gets a supply of drugs I'm pretty fucking sure she bought with her salary, with the intent to sell. What Dedra's dumb self don't know, is that I'm pretty certain the same dude that sold her those drugs was the very same dude who snitched so the cops could raid our apartment and find the drugs. Because there were so many dirty cops, he probably had the dope boy working for him, so when he makes his drug bust he turns right around and gives the dope boy back his supply. Which is what happened to my girl.

Imagine my surprise when my door gets kicked in and this cop finds a stash of drugs hidden in our apartment. I swear to god, if those police weren't around, and I had found those drugs my damn self, Dedra would be floating down a river somewhere. How stupid can you be, to bring that quantity of drugs in your apartment with kids in it? What if one of the kids had found that shit and thought it was candy and had taken it. Can't even think what that would have been like.

So when the drugs was found I did the only thing I could do to save my kids the trauma of seeing their mother being taken away in handcuffs: I lied and said the drugs were mine. I don't regret it though; I did what I had to do. But now, a nigga getting tired as fuck being in this prison. First couple weeks of being in here I got into it with this clown ass nigga who thought I was some lame. Those little bruises Dedra saw on my face was nothing compared to what I did to homeboy.

"Aye, look at this pussy tryna make a jump shot," Cedric said, clowning at one of the inmates whose three-point shot sailed clear over the basketball ring. You would think these niggas would be able to ball after being locked up for so long; not the case though.

"Look who just showed up; it's your homeboy J," Steve said as he lightly tapped me on my arm. I turned in the direction he was looking at, and walking into the open area was one of the prison officers. This officer right here was the reason I didn't get thrown in the hole when I got into my fight when I first got here. He said I had all rights to defend myself or I would have gotten stabbed if I didn't. That last part wasn't true, but nobody had to know that.

As he looked over in my direction, he signaled with a slight head nod letting me know he wanted to holla at me. I told Cedric and Steve I would be right back and jogged over to where he stood.

"What's up big Justin." Mothafucker was wider than all of outside; don't even know how he got this damn job with his big ass.

"Just now got on my shift here; hoping it's gonna be a nice, quiet day for me." We both chuckled at his statement, because it would be anything but quiet.

"But listen up; I got some news for you man." I creased my forehead as I waited for him to continue.

"Word is, the last judge, you know the one who was on duty when that big ass brawl broke out." I shook my head in recollection. Because of that stupid ass fight breaking out, my case got pushed back till I don't have a clue when.

"Well word on the street is, that judge got caught in some sort of scandal." My head turned to look at him so fast, it damn near fell off.

"Scandal! What kind of scandal?" I narrowed my eyes as I looked at him.

"Man something about prostitutes and midgets." I hollered out laughing, because this fool was wilding right now, talking 'bout midgets.

"Anyway, forget all that. So the judge gets kicked out of the court right, so they appoint this new judge; now the thing about this new judge is that he gives zero fucks." His voice got real low as if he was about to tell me a secret.

"So this judge decides he's gonna throw out cases that he considers minor cases. Says he's not here to waste time on no bullshit, petty charges. So guess what nigga?" I had kinda been bored of this conversation a few seconds now, so I had turned my attention back to the basketball game, which by the way seemed a lot rougher than before.

"Guess nigga!" Justin's big ass shouted at me. I looked back at him and shrugged my shoulders, twisting my face a bit.

"Word is, your case was one of those cases that mothafucker threw out." My jaw dropped almost hitting my chest. What in the fuck?

"What did you just say?" He now had my full attention as I turned to him.

"That's what I thought; you listening now right. Yup, your case got thrown out. Consider yourself lucky with that amount of drugs they found in the apartment. But it looks like the fact that you never got in any type of trouble with the law played a huge part in his decision. If you're lucky, you could be out of here by tomorrow." It was like I was hearing what he was saying to me, but the shit just wasn't registering.

"Hey, are sure you know what you're talking about man?" My heart started beating fast in my chest with excitement of the realization that I could be a free man, going home to my family...finally!!

"Word is my bond. I wouldn't speak on it if I didn't know what I was talking about." I smiled a very wide smile; I was ecstatic!

"Aye fuck you nigga; your foot was on the line!" Shouts from the basketball game suddenly had our attention, as two of the guys playing were suddenly in each other's faces. And without warning, one of them swung on the other hitting him square in his face. Next thing you know, the whole fucking yard is fighting.

"Hey! Hey! Break it the fuck up!" Justin's big self attempted to sprint across to the brawl, but by then other officers were racing over, batons in hand, just swinging at mothafuckers. I kept a safe distance. What did I say? Before y'all came to the end of this chapter a fight was gonna break out! I looked on as the officers struggled to quell the situation, but my mind kept going back to what Justin said. If he was right...I'm about to be a free man pretty soon!

CHAPTER TWO

Jamal

Guess Who's Back?

"Ow! The fuck are you trying to do, make my injuries worse?" I snatched the medicine kit from out of her hands; bitches could never do anything right I swear.

"Well excuse me for trying to help your ass. I told you how many times to leave that bitch anyways." I ought to bop her in her head for saying something like that about my wife.

"Aye, watch yo' mothafuckin' mouth talking about my wife and the mother of my kids like that before I punch you in your throat." That shut her ass up real quick; she turned and walked off in the direction of the bathroom. I watched her disappear before I started thinking what was going to be my next plan of action.

I was nursing so many bruises and a couple of broken bones, after that stupid mothafucker showed up at my job and took me for a mothafucking trunk ride, and beat the shit out of me.

Then that nigga had the nerve to tell me to stay away from my wife…MY WIFE. How the hell another nigga gone tell you to stay away from your own mothafuckin' wife?? If that ain't some bullshit, I don't know what the fuck is! So I've been hiding out at my ole girl's apartment in downtown Brooklyn until I'm all healed, and then I'm gonna go get my mothafuckin' wife back. Not that I want her stupid ass or nothing, but for the fact that she obviously had a side nigga all this time. Who the fuck does Avion think she is cheating on me?!

I should have killed her the last time I beat her ass.

One problem though, the nigga she messing on me with... I know that fool.

However, he has no idea who I am!

"Do you want me to make you something to eat?" I groaned silently as I looked over my shoulder at her, because she knew I was going to say yes.

"You know I want something to eat; don't know why you even asking." I sucked my teeth loudly at her, turning my back once again as she left the room. I sat on the bed and began brainstorming about what I needed to do. I couldn't just run up on Avion letting her know she was coming back with me. Nah that would be too risky; because I definitely didn't want that nigga finding out I was still in Brooklyn after he warned me to leave.

I had to be sneaky about my shit. By now the landlord probably had already evicted her ass on account of I stopped paying the rent. I had to use that money for my own personal shit. Besides, I knew what Avion would do. She would take the kids over to her grandma's house and she would probably just kick it over at that bitch Dedra's house. I couldn't stand that bitch. She was always filling Avion's head with bullshit; with her ho ass.

As soon as I think I could move about freely without being in too much pain, I was going to stalk her stupid ass; Avion got me all the way fucked up! Fucking another nigga all this goddamn time behind my back. I wish I could confess to that nigga who the fuck I am just to see the look on his face. But he would probably blow my brains out the back of my head; I didn't need to die just yet. Sometimes I want to be a good husband and father to my kids, but then I remember what Avion did, and that feeling goes away like I took a mouthful of Pepto Bismol.

My kids are cool and all, but let's face it: I'm a terrible father just like I suck as a husband. But that doesn't mean I'm gonna leave Avion to spread her legs for the next nigga; hell na!

Giving myself about a week, I'll continue to lay low for now; but within the next few days Avion is going to get taught a lesson!

CHAPTER THREE

Ummm Who's Chyna???

I passed my hands through my silky 18" Brazilian weave as I sat in the back seat of the taxi making my way to the condos in Manhattan. I looked down at my expensive Chanel handbag, my expensive designer outfit and newly manicured nails and smiled to myself.

So who am I? Well, I'm Tremaine's girlfriend of course; you know the one who left a few years ago with our son to find herself. Yeah, that one. So I was on my way back to get my man. I mean people do make mistakes right? And I realize now that I was wrong to leave with our son without letting him know where I was going; I could admit that now, but I have learned my lesson.

I really didn't mean to leave Tremaine the way I did, but it just seemed that his life wasn't going anywhere. He used to kick it back in the day with that brother of his, who ended up getting killed. Tremaine was about that street life when we met, and back then that sort of thing really appealed to me; but then it started to get boring and lame, and I needed a change. Even though Tremaine did manage to get a regular job after his brother's passing, his earnings were so meager though. I mean how could you keep a woman like me satisfied with a basic job and a basic salary? Then he gets arrested for however long, I find out I'm pregnant while he's locked up, then he gets out and comes up with this ridiculous idea to sue the state.

I'm like, nigga that suing the shit only works for white people! While he was locked up I met somebody, and he didn't care that I was pregnant for another nigga. So I decided to leave to give me and my son the type of lifestyle I believed we deserved.

But that asshole that I ran off with to Michigan was just a waste anyway. He made me believe he was rolling in all this cash when he really wasn't about that million dollar lifestyle, and I am a very expensive female to maintain. My returning had nothing to do with the fact that I found out that Tremaine is now a millionaire! When I left he was in the process of suing. I had told him suing would take years, and he probably wouldn't even win his case. I left before his case even started, so imagine my surprise when I found out that he won and now owns a very successful car rental company.

"Sit up straight baby, don't slouch. You know mummy doesn't like it when you slouch." I spoke to my son who quickly did what he was told; it's kind of eerie the way he looks exactly like his father. Tremaine would be so happy to see his son; I know how much he absolutely adored him.

I wasn't worried about any relationship Tremaine may be involved in. If it was one thing I learned about that man, was that family came first. So whatever little flavor of the week he had entertaining him while I was gone, was about to be a thing of the past.

Because the boss bitch was back!

CHAPTER FOUR

Avion

Mixed Emotions

I was laid out on the couch trying my best to get some sleep, but it was damn near impossible. My mind kept going back to Stormy's crazy ass, and the nerve of Dedra to actually think it's a good idea! Who those bitches think we are? Thelma and Louise? Stormy had left a while ago and Dedra was in her room asleep I guess. She came and tried to convince me this whole robbery thing was actually a good idea; I mean I know Richard is loaded and all, and I also know he's a pretty shitty father to his daughter. But that does not mean we just grab up some guns and go rob the fool!

"Uggh!" I groaned as I turned awkwardly on Dedra's small ass couch; shit was uncomfortable as hell. I had to think about what I was gonna do in terms of getting myself a new apartment. I can't just continue living off my friend. I know Tremaine gave me the keys to his place out in Newark, but that was kind of far from where my kids go to school; plus that's not my house. I sighed loudly at the fine hell of a predicament I was now faced with. One thing I knew for sure was that I was not about to rob nobody!

Maybe I could ask Dedra if she would mind if I could do a few people's hair over here at her apartment. I mean I could more than use the money, and she could even assist a little and we share whatever I made, seeing that her ass was now unemployed and all. It's way better than grabbing a gun and thinking to stick up a nigga.

Stormy and Avion are crazy as hell if they thinking they could get away with that kind of bullshit. But, I don't think they would have the guts to go through with it anyway. I mean to rob somebody is a well thought out, organized type of crime; these two bitches could never even show up on time if we plan a date to the movies. I wasn't too worried. I believed they would eventually realize that they just talking crazy, and would eventually give up on the idea of robbing Richard once they see how ridiculous their plan is.

My mind suddenly began thinking of Jamal. I mean suppose something has really happened to him? He wouldn't just leave his job like that; he was way too committed. I wonder if I should make some sort of report to the police, like a missing person's report or something. No matter how awful Jamal had been to me in the past, he was still my children's father. It was irrelevant in my book if he wanted to be found or not. His kids deserved to know where their father was. Taking my phone from under the pillow my head was on, I dialed his number like I had done so many times since finding out he was missing. But the phone never even rang, just went straight to voicemail.

I wasn't so sure what to make of Jamal's sudden disappearance;

it could be that he's scared that he hurt me so bad from when he last put his hands on me. Or could simply be that he left me; he just left me to stand alone on my two feet without a dime to my name, with my kids depending on me. *Death must be easy, because life sure is hard,* I thought to myself as I dialed Tremaine's number without putting too much thought into it.

"Hello," he answered sounding as if he had a mouthful of food or something. I can't even lie, Tremaine's fine, freaky self gave that business to me so damn good when I was over at his place in Newark; had a bitch talking in tongues. He did things to me, touched places I didn't know could turn me on, hit spots in my pussy that instantly had me gushing all over his dick. Oh my god! It was heavenly. Now I knew what I was missing all these years messing with Jamal's selfish ass; I was never going back!

"What you up to 'Tre?" I smiled as I listened to him chew noisily into the phone.

"Doing some damage to a bowl of Trix." I shook my head at his response, because Tremaine's grown ass is always eating that damn cereal. That's what he was getting when we first met that day in the supermarket.

"You and that damn cereal. Anyway babe let me tell you something real quick about Stormy and Dedra." I took my voice level down a couple notches as I was about to spill the tea.

"Hol'up baby, somebody knocking at my door. Don't know who the hell tryna holla at this time of night; almost midnight." I listened as he moved around making his way to his front door as I was also curious as to who would be visiting him so late.

"What the fuck." That was the last thing I heard before Tremaine's call suddenly got disconnected. Removing the phone from my ear, because I was unsure if he just hung up on me, I looked at the screen. And sure enough, the screen was back to my home screen.

"What the hell made him hang up the phone?" I asked out loud as I tried dialing his number again, but it just rang out. I tried one more time, and this time he answered.

"Avi I'm dealing with something; gimme a few minutes." Before I even had the time to answer, the phone went dead again; like what the hell! Tremaine had better have an excellent explanation on why he thought it was cool to hang the phone up on me.

I laid the phone on top of my chest as I waited patiently on Tremaine to call me back; unfortunately…he never did!

CHAPTER FIVE

Tremaine

My Eyes Are Playing Tricks On Me

*I*f my heart started beating any faster, it would burst through my ribcage, I swear. Standing at my door was Chyna, and next to her was the most handsome lil" nigga I've ever seen. He was trying to hide behind her as he shyly looked up at me.

"What the fuck." I didn't mean for the expletive to leave my lips, but a nigga was shocked as hell right about now; so excuse my language.

"Hi babyyy." Chyna all but threw herself into me, as she wrapped her arms tightly around my neck. I couldn't even move; just stood there like a tree as she continued on with her tight embrace. I heard my phone ringing in my hand, but I couldn't get to answering it with Chyna hanging on to my neck the way she was.

Finally, she released me and looked at me with a big ass smile on her lips, as if she hadn't vanish into thin air for the past three and a half years.

"What…where you come from Chyna?" I asked her as she took a

hold of our son's hand, bringing him to stand in front of her.

"Well aren't you gonna invite us into your lovely condo?" she asked as she peeped her head in, her eyes roaming all over, taking in my place. Moving to the side so that I could allow them to walk in, my phone started ringing again.I knew it would have been Avion, and I answered promptly.

"Avi I'm dealing with something; gimme a few minutes." I spoke quickly into the phone and then hung it up as I watched my son sitting on my sectional, eyes wide looking at me with curiosity. *Man he looked just like me too,* I thought as I smiled, walking over to have a seat.

I just sat there, looking from my son then back to Chyna as I waited patiently for her to explain where the fuck she been at all this mothafucking time!

"Look, baby I know you probably got a million and twenty questions, but we are so tired all we wanna do is lay down and sleep." This chick must be mental. She's acting like she just got back from the mall or something and not that she's been gone for years.

"Chyna, are you serious right now! Chyna where the hell have you been with my son all this time? Then you waltz in here as if you don't owe me some type of explanation as to why you just decided to do a disappearing act with my seed!" Yeah, so I was beginning to get a little upset; my voice went up a couple levels.

"I would prefer not to have this conversation in front of him. Can you put him to lay down somewhere at least?" Looking over at my lil" man, my heart burst with pride because he looked like me so much. I got up and made my way over to where he sat, but I stopped short in my tracks when I saw him cower away from me. Not wanting him to be afraid of me anymore than he obviously was, I turned to Chyna.

"Maybe you should take him; he don't really know me like that." I gave her a side glance, hoping she got where I was coming from as I returned to my seat. Standing up with Trevelle's hand in hers, I pointed her in the direction of my bedroom and watched as she walked away with my son.

Rubbing my palms against my face harshly, I felt like I was in some sort of dream. I literally put my fingers on my thigh and pinched myself…hard! This shit was unbelievable. Who the fuck does crazy shit like this? Chyna was a certified nut case for real.

Looking up as I heard her footsteps, I watched as she made her way over to me, taking a seat next to me as she turned to face me, smiling seductively.

Nah, fuck that. "You got a lot of fucking nerve Chyna." I clenched my teeth, trying my best not to make any kind of eye contact with her; because I felt like if I did, I may very well punch her lights out. And I pride myself on being a calm nigga that don't hit women.

"You just waltz up in my shit, with my son you disappeared with, not so much of a fucking word, or a fucking call. And you sit here looking at me with a big muthafuckin' smile on your face." I shook my head as the words passed my lips. Chyna reached for my hand, and I pulled back instantly.

"Look, Tremaine you have all rights to be upset with me, but I was younger back then." I looked at her then, because I knew that was bullshit. "But baby, I've changed now; and I'm ready to be a good woman to you, the kind you want. I'm ready for us to be a family." I'm sitting here looking at this lunatic, thinking I had a child with a crazy person and just now knew it.

"Chyna, don't try to play me. Who the fuck was he? Hmmm... what was his name? I know you Chyna; you only look out for yourself, nobody else." I got up and stood in front of her, bending a little to get all in her face. Because I wanted to make sure she heard everything I was about to tell her ass.

"So what? That nigga dump you? Don't want your ass no more? Oh no, wait, did his money run out?" I saw her eye twitch just then, and laughed hysterically.

"So that's it. That nigga's money done ran out, and what? You thought you'd just come back home to me and I'd just take your stupid ass back? You must be delusional. As soon as day breaks, take your shit and get the fuck up out my apartment. But you're leaving my son." My face was mere inches from hers after I got everything I wanted to tell her off my chest.

And Chyna, being Chyna...she did what she always do when somebody was telling her ass the truth that she couldn't handle. She started with the water works.

"I'm sorry Tre," she said in between her fake crying. I decided to amuse myself so I stood upright and listened. "I wanted to call you so many times, but that nigga was so controlling. He didn't want me being in contact with you or any of my family members." She sniffed dramatically as she wiped her tears.

"He even threatened to hurt Trevelle, so I did what I had to, to protect myself and my baby." Looking down at her, I didn't believe a word of what her conniving ass had just said. I decided it was way too late for all this bullshit, and decided to call it a night. I would deal with Chyna first thing in the morning.

"You can sleep on the bed with Trevelle; I'll sleep in the other bedroom," I said softly to her. The way my mind set up right now, I couldn't deal with all of this presently.

Standing, Chyna stood directly in front of me, and without warning she tip-toed and kissed my cheek. "I just want for us to be a family again; I didn't mean to upset you. Thank you for allowing us to stay at your lovely condo." Her hand caressed my upper arm before she turned and walked off in the direction of my room.

God was testing me! I was convinced that God was testing a nigga. A test that I was uncertain I was ready for, I thought to myself as I made my way to my bedroom. My mind was so far gone I hadn't even realized I didn't return Avion's phone call.

CHAPTER SIX

Stormy

No Dick For Stormy

I was back in my apartment with Racine in my arms. My mind definitely on overdrive, I knew Avion and Dedra were probably thinking I was some sort of mental case; but I wasn't...I was just a female that was tired. I was tired of Richard and his lying ways, and his constant lack of claiming responsibility for Racine. Our daughter was sick, and all this asshole could say was that he don't make sick babies.

Looking down at my baby as she lay quietly in my arms gnawing away at her fist, I smiled lovingly down at her as she looked up at me with her piercing blue eyes.

"Don't worry baby, momma got you," I whispered to her as I kissed the top of her head. I kept her in my arms until she fell asleep and gently placed her in her crib. It was time to start planning this shit. We had a certain amount of time we were going to do this, and certain things needed to be put in place as soon as possible.

Taking a seat in my living room, I sat and started thinking about all that we needed, because I was determined to pull this off with just us. We didn't need anybody else; we could do this shit, and if Avion didn't wish to be down, then fuck her. More money for me and Dedra to split between us two, that's all.

Grabbing my phone beside me, I needed my mind to focus on something different, so I pulled up Xavier's number. I haven't spoken to him since his little stunt he pulled at his barbershop, so I decided to call him and see what he got going on.

I dialed his number and waited patiently for him to answer. "Stormy?" was all he said after four rings.

"Why you took so long to answer Xavier, you didn't wanna talk to me?" My defenses were already up, and we didn't even started talking yet.

"Man Stormy, don't start with all that noise. What you want?" I sighed into the phone.

"Can you come see me? I got something I need to talk to you about," I said, as I waited quietly for his reply, hoping he wouldn't cuss me out.

I heard him suck his teeth at me. "I'm not coming over there to give you no dick so just forget it." *Vain ass nigga,* I thought while rolling my eyes at his reply.

"Ain't nobody tryna ride your dick Xavier!" His stupid self had me regretting that I called his annoying ass in the first place. "Something is wrong with Racine; I just wanted to tell you about it." He annoyed me so much I just decided to hang up the phone, didn't even want to talk to him no more.

Throwing the phone on the sofa, I got up and marched into my small kitchen to see what I could cook. Sometimes when I'm in a bad mood, cooking relaxes me somehow. Opening my refrigerator and going through the shelves, I realized I needed to make groceries, which was ironic seeing that a bitch works in a grocery store. Shaking my head, I just decided to make some mac and cheese.

About twenty minutes after I'm sitting Indian style on my sofa, hot plate of food in my hand, when my phone started ringing next to me. Looking down at the screen and seeing Xavier's name pop up, I sucked my teeth and hit the ignore button.

"Fuck boy, ain't nobody wanna talk to your ass," I said to the empty apartment as I pushed a forkful of cheesy macaroni in my mouth.

BANG! BANG! BANG!

The loudest knocks at my door vibrated loudly, making me jump to the point where my food almost fell out my hand.

"The fuck," I said, putting the bowl down and getting up to see who it was about to get cussed the hell out.

"Don't make me break this door in Stormy!" Xavier shouted just as I had my hand on the door knob. Opening the door, pulling on it so hard I almost knocked my own self in the head, I stood glaring at him.

"So, you ignoring my calls Stormy." He pointed his finger in my face, and I swear I almost bit that fucker.

"What you want X?" I looked him up and down, trying to keep my voice down so my nosey neighbors wouldn't be tempted to call the police.

CANDY MOORE

"Oh you don't want this dick?" he said as he thrust his hips upward into me. I couldn't suppress the giggle that escaped my lips.

"You are such a child X…I swear." I continued laughing, as he made no move to release my wrists.

"Tell me you like me." His face serious all of a sudden as he looked at me intensely.

Tilting my head to one side, I said, "You know I like you, stupid." This reply brought a bright, wide smile to his face. All I wore was an oversized T-shirt and no bra, with a pair of lace thong underwear. And all I was doing right now was wishing I had more clothes on, as Xavier scanned over my body greedily with his eyes.

"Tell me you want me in your life." His voice was now low and husky. Shifting my wrists so now they only were imprisoned by one of his hands, he used the free hand to roam up my thigh.

Our eyes were locked with each other's, as his hand continued up my thigh, slowly making its way to my pussy, that had been wet since this nigga walked through my front door.

"Tell me Stormy, tell me you gonna let a nigga in." After saying the word in, he slipped his middle finger inside of me, causing me gasp out loud as I threw my head back, loving the way that it felt.

"Tell me…" His finger started making slow lazy circles around my clit, and my body reacted instinctively as I grinded against his hand, low moans escaping my lips.

"I can't hear you Stormy." He made slow circles, then quickened the pace, and I felt like I was about to lose my fucking mind. As if my mouth were somehow being puppeteered by some unseen force, I replied to him.

"Yes, I'll be in your life. I want you in my life Xavier." Apparently that was all he wanted to hear as he literally ripped my underwear off and reached inside of his sweat pants and pulled his solid, rock hard dick out.

"What were you saying about not riding my dick?" Smiling at me in an evil fashion, he held his dick upright. I tugged at my hand that he still held as prisoner, until he let it go. Positioning myself over him, I slowly glided his dick inside me, moaning loudly as I did.

"Fuck! Xavier I missed you," I shamelessly admitted as he placed his hand on my ass and rocked me back and forth, feeling him deep inside of me.

"Fuck me like you missed me then." Shit! He didn't have to tell me twice. Placing my hands on his shoulders, I eased myself up until I was in a squatting position. I bounced up and down on his dick until that nigga was begging me to stop, saying he'll cum too quick in it.

I worked his pipe relentlessly, enjoying every minute that he grunted and moaned out my name.

All I kept thinking was that I really meant what I said. I wanted Xavier in my life; he balances the crazy in me.

CHAPTER SEVEN

Avion

I always pride myself on being a level-headed, calm woman. Even when Jamal used to have his way, beating me to a bloody pulp, I still somehow managed to keep a level head. But all that level-headed shit was about to get tossed out the fucking window as I stood in front of Tremaine's condo, about to knock on his door.

He said he would call me back, but for whatever reason he never did. And then this morning I decided I would give him a call to find out what the hell was going, only for his phone to go straight to voicemail. I had no idea what was happening, but I for damn sure was about to find out.

So I managed to convince Dedra to bring me over to his place, and here I am standing in front of his door, hand about to knock, when I began saying to myself, *what the fuck am I doing?* I mean really, Tremaine owes me no explanation. Not like he's my man or nothing. I decided I should stop trippin' and was about to leave, when I heard what sounded like someone moving around in the kitchen.

"Fuck it, I'm already here." I gave myself a quick pep talk and knocked on his door. I stood and waited, hearing the sound of footsteps…quiet footsteps approaching. The door swung open, and a bitch had to look at the number on the door real quick. Because I believed I had the wrong apartment.

Because instead of a handsome, chocolate brother standing here, it was some random hoochie, long weave in her hair, wearing nothing but a barely there T-shirt and barefooted.

"Yes, can I help you?" She had the nerve to eyeball me up and down, like I was the one out of place for being at Tremaine's apartment.

"Yeah, for starters you could tell Tremaine bring his ass!" I felt myself getting worked up, wanting to scream in this bitch's face to move out my way.

Snapping her neck back and this time taking her time to scan me over once more, she smiled slowly as she folded her arms under her breast. Breasts, by the way, that weren't hidden in a bra. Her nipples were straining against the thin material of her T-shirt.

"Do you know who I am?" she asked with a sly smile still on her lips.

"I don't give a fuck who you are. Is Tremaine here or not?" My chest started feeling tight, my anxiety taking over completely.

"Oh, he's here, but he's asleep. He had a long night, if you know what I mean," she said as she licked her lips. I think I'm about to headbutt this bitch!

As I was about to tell her to go fuck herself, I took a good look at her; and I realized just who she was. In the photo Tremaine had with her, her hair was much shorter; this was Tremaine's baby momma that stood before me. *Where in the fuck did she come from?*

"What? Did you think what you and Tremaine had was real? You thought he was in love or some shit?" She chuckled, shaking her head as she unfolded her arms and placed her hand on the door knob. "Please, I have his son, his one and only child. What the fuck do you have for him? That old worn out kitty?"

"Tremaine will call it off with you faster than he could finish a bowl of cereal. So whatever you thought y'all had, you could just go right ahead and forget about it."

Looking like she felt real proud of her little speech she just gave, she folded her arms once again as she stared at me.

I felt really dumb right about now. Here I thought that maybe Tremaine was probably sick or something, and that's why he hadn't gotten back in contact with me. Come to find out that he wasn't returning my call because his baby momma had somehow managed to wiggle her way back in.

As I was about to tell her she could have Tremaine's ass so I could turn and leave, Hhere comes this nigga walking out from his bedroom, rubbing his eyes, wearing nothing but a pair of black sweat pants. My jaw tightened as he looked up at me and froze in his tracks; seems as though he didn't know exactly what he should do.

"Avion, how long have you been here?" Looking like a straight up punk, he kept looking at me, then back at his baby momma as though he was trying to find the right words to say.

"And here I thought you were different," I said with my jaw tight, as I narrowed my eyes at him. "Turns out you, ain't no better, just full of shit like everybody else." Turning to his *girlfriend*, I smiled at her. "You can go ahead and have his lying ass." Giving Tremaine one final death glare, I turned and stormed off towards the elevator.

"Avion! Avion!" Like hell I was going to turn around and deal with his lies and half-truths. Just as I reached the elevator and was about to hit the button, I felt Tremaine roughly grab me by my arm, turning me around to face him.

"Where the fuck you think you're going Avion?" I was breathing heavily, pure rage taking over my senses. I pulled out of his hold with such force, I almost knocked my own self in the face.

"Don't you fucking touch me after you were probably fucking your baby momma all night!" I screamed at him. Taking my hand, I swung at him hitting his upper arm. "She the reason why you couldn't return my call, hung up the phone on me, your phone switched the fuck off taking me to voicemail?!" I continued shouting at him, while all he did was stare at me.

"First off, don't ever think it's ok to put your motherfucking hands on me. Second, I'm just as shocked as you to see Chyna; she just showed up with our son. I couldn't just turn my back on them, let them leave to roam the streets, so I told her to stay. I slept in the other bedroom. So chill the fuck out and come back inside." Maybe he was telling the truth, maybe he was lying. But one thing's for certain.... I was a third wheel. How could I possibly compete with this chick? I'm pretty sure he still had feelings for her, pretty sure if he had to choose, he would choose her. Who was I kidding?

Sighing softly, I reached into my jeans pocket and pulled the key for the house out in Newark, placing it in the palm of his hand. I turned around and hit the elevator button.

"Why the fuck are you giving me this Avion?" I dared not turn to face him, just hoping the elevator would hurry the fuck up so that I could be out. Tremaine wasn't having me ignoring him, so he placed his hand on my shoulder and turned me around to face him.

"You deaf? Why are giving me back the keys that I gave to you?

"Tremaine, look at us; we are not even really in a relationship and we already at each other's throats. We can't do this; we can't try to make this work." He took a step back from me after I said those words.

"With that type of negative thinking how in the fuck do you expect it to? Can't you see how much I like you? How much I want to be with you?" he said as he pointed from me back to himself.

"How do you expect this to work Tremaine? How?" I shouted back at him, because really I was so over this. And why the fuck is this goddamn elevator taking so long? "I think you should just go on ahead and make things work with your baby—I mean with Chyna."

"Man, I don't give a fuck what you think. You think I'm not a grown ass man to know who and what the fuck I want Avi!" Finally the elevator reached our floor and opened, and I stepped inside eagerly.

"If you think I'll just let you walk the fuck out my life, you're dead ass wrong." We stared at each other for the couple of seconds it took for the elevator door to close. As soon it started its descent, I let out a sigh of relief, or was it frustration? Either way I had to figure out what my next move would be; time felt like it was quickly running out. I barely had any money, and my kids were living in a one bedroom apartment with my grandmother. This shit was a nightmare.

As the doors opened and I walked out heading to where Dedra was parked, I began thinking about what they were thinking about doing to Richard. And the more I thought about it, bit by bit I was beginning to think maybe it wasn't such a bad idea.

CHAPTER EIGHT

Dedra

Daddy's Home

"Girl, I swear to you I am not lying." I sat on my small sofa in my apartment, giving Stormy the tea over the phone that Avion might just be down with what we were planning to do.

"So what the fuck made her change her mind?" Stormy was sounding happy as hell that all of us were now in on her plan.

"Girl, that nigga Tremaine. Guess what?" I waited for her to play my little guessing game, which she didn't do.

"Guess bitch!" I yelled into the phone at her ass. She sucked her teeth loudly at me.

"I don't have time for this shit, just tell me how it went down Dedra." Stormy was no fun, I swear.

"Well, it seems that nigga had a whole family. I'm talking about a whole baby momma, and a whole boy child." Stormy groaned loudly at what I just revealed.

"So Avion's dumb self said she knew about them, but he told her that she left a couple years ago with the baby, and now she's back to get her man. I told her ass, his baby momma probably never left; you know how niggas lie."

"If it's anybody who knows that first hand, it's me," Stormy said, obviously talking about Richard. "I feel bad for her though Dedra. I mean first, Jamal done did a disappearing act on her, and now this fool got baby momma drama." I shook my head, because it was like Avion couldn't catch a break; none of us actually.

"So she gave that nigga back the keys to his house, and she's tryna brainstorm on how she could get some money to start a new life with her and the kids. So I know she's down." I smiled from ear to ear, because us three we needed this to work.

"Where is she anyway?" I got up from the sofa as I prepared to organize the apartment a bit, because pretty soon I would have a visitor.

"She took the kids to the park. Benjamin about to come over," I said quickly, hoping Stormy wouldn't hear my words properly.

"Wait, wait, hold up...did you just say Benjamin is about to come over? Bitch! You a ho; you about to fuck your baby daddy's lawyer." Stormy fell out laughing loudly in my ear, which only pissed me off.

"Shut the fuck up Stormy. Ain't nobody about to fuck Benjamin. Besides, something's going on with Dornell." I sighed loudly, taking a seat on the sofa once again.

"What you mean? Is he alright? When is his next hearing?" Stormy rattled off a bunch of questions that I actually had no answers to, because my man refused to see me!

"Stormy, I don't know what the fuck Dornell's problem is. I've tried to visit him the past couple days, and he told the officer to let me know he's not accepting any visitors." I didn't know what my man's problem was, but I was determined to find out.

"Do you think he was in a fight or something, and doesn't want you to see his bruises?" That thought actually did cross my mind, and I was hoping I was wrong.

"Girl, I hope not. Thing is he's refusing to see Benjamin also. How the fuck is he going to refuse to see his own goddamn lawyer. So I told Benjamin come over so we could brainstorm and try and figure out what the fuck should be done about my stupid man." Stormy chuckled, but my face remained hard as stone, because Dornell was irking the hell out of me, I swear.

"Anyway, I'm about to go. X is coming over. Don't forget we have to meet up and talk, aight. You, me and Avion." I shook my head, as if she could actually see. Truth was, I couldn't believe what we were actually considering doing.

"How's lil' mama doing?" I enquired about Racine, the reason for our crazy plan. Stormy and I talked about Racine and her condition until I heard a knock at my door and told her I had to go.

"Ok, so tomorrow we'll meet up, aight." I agreed before quickly hanging up the phone and getting up to open the door. As I was about to swing the door open, I decided to give myself a quick scan, making sure the thin strapped, long, baby pink maxi dress I wore fell nicely on my body. Dedra you trippin', I thought to myself as I rolled my eyes and opened the door.

Well damn! Benjamin stood in the doorway looking like a whole snack—I kid you not. This may have been the first time I saw his fine self in a pair of blue jeans, navy blue ones. I don't know exactly what brand of jeans it was, but it hugged his toned legs perfectly. And the white, long sleeved sweater he wore hugged all the right muscles.

"You done eye raping me? You really need to get some. Can I come in?" I wasn't even sure if that was a question or not; because I didn't even have time to respond before he just barged his way into my apartment. Well y'all already knew he was rude, so his attitude shouldn't come as a surprise.

"Sure, you can come in Benjamin," I said sarcastically, as I closed the door with a shake of my head.

"Has your man tried to get in contact with you as yet?" he asked as he sat at the edge of my sofa, placing his hands on his knees as his eyes followed me, as I took a seat next to him.

"No, he hasn't, and he's beginning to piss me the hell off too!" As I sat next to him, his cologne invaded my senses, hypnotizing me a bit.

"Look, I think there's something you should know." He turned his body in my direction, as he slowly brushed his fingers on his nice, full, suckable…um, forget that last part. He passed his fingers on his full lips.

"What's that?" I held my breath expecting to hear the worst. Maybe Dornell was dead! Maybe that's why I haven't heard from him; maybe the prison was trying to cover it up. Putting trembling fingers up to my mouth, I waited for what he was about to say.

"The hell is wrong with you Dedra? Why you sitting there

trembling like you got nerves?" Benjamin looked totally confused at my behavior.

"He's dead isn't he?" I blurted out as I covered my eyes, waiting for Benjamin to give his confirmation of my worst thoughts.

"Dead! The hell is wrong with you, why you putting that man in his grave before his time with your dramatic ass?" I sat up, removing my hands away from my face as I stared at Benjamin.

"That nigga ain't dead? Well then he's about to wish he was dead. Why the fuck is he refusing to see us?" Forget feeling scared, now I was mad all over again! What the fuck was Dornell's problem anyway?

"Would you calm it all the way down and let me say what I came to say? Damn."

"Ok fine, go ahead Benjamin," I replied with a twist of my neck. I couldn't help but give him a little sass.

"Look, word is, the judge who was working Dornell's and a few other cases, got kicked out over some scandal." Not really being too surprised, I waited for him to get to the point, because the most amount of corrupted people always held high ranking positions, if you ask me. "Anyway, so they appointed a new judge, who obviously don't have time for no bullshit. He started throwing cases out left to right. And after doing some investigating, I found out that Dornell's case was one of the cases he trashed." I started blinking rapidly, as if something was in my eye.

"What! What did you just say?" I whispered to him, because I had to be dreaming.

Big smile on his face, he reached out and took a hold of my

hand, "Yup, he's going to be a free man. Thanks to the fact that he has a squeaky clean record." I started smiling so hard at Benjamin my cheeks hurt.

"So when is he getting out? Oh my god, I'm so happy. Thank goodness." I breathed out a long, loud sigh of relief. My man was about to come home y'all!

"See that's the thing, I don't know. It could be any day from what I gather. Because he refuses to see me or you, I have no way of knowing. I think maybe he's just holding out to surprise you, that he found out that he was about to be a free man and is just keeping it to himself; I dunno." I could just kiss Benjamin; this has been the best news I've heard in a minute.

"Benjamin, I swear I don't know how to thank you," I said softly, as I covered his hand that was holding mine, with my other hand, and looked deeply into his eyes.

"Well for starters," he cleared his throat and leaned forward, towards me, "I'll take the rest of my payment." We both laughed, because really I had to find a way to pay the man. "But for now, a hug will do." Feeling myself blush like some lovesick school girl, I nodded my head in a positive response, and we both leaned into each other for our embrace.

Wrapping my arms tightly around his neck, inhaling deeply the sensuous smell of his obviously expensive cologne, I enjoyed the feel of a strong, protective hug from the opposite sex; it's been a while.

"You feel so good," Benjamin said against my ear, his breath smelling as though he may have just had a cup of coffee before coming over. Benjamin and I clearly were enjoying our little sofa embrace a little too much.

Because we were so caught up in each other, we didn't even hear the door open and close, until it was too fucking late.

"So you ain't hear from a nigga in a couple of days, and you bring this nigga up in my crib?" Letting out a startled gasp, I pulled away from Benjamin and turned to the front door to see none other than Dornell standing there, his hands balled in a fist.

And where in the fuck did he come from? I thought to myself as I watched him tighten his jaw in anger. Now I knew my man, and that look on his face said it all. I got up slowly to make my way over to him, to explain what he saw was completely innocent.

But before I made a good three steps, Dornell was airborne, lunging towards Benjamin.

"You a disrespectful ass nigga!" Was all I heard before fists were seen flying in rage!

CHAPTER NINE

Chyna

Chyna's Wrath

Tremaine really liked that bitch, I could tell. He was practically stalking her phone, he kept calling her over and over; but she never answered. I was in the kitchen cooking up some breakfast, as I listened attentively as he sat cursing under his breath at the fact that Avion was ignoring the fuck outta him. I would love to know where in the hell that bitch came from to have Tremaine all in his feelings and shit. I'll be damned, however, if some random hood bitch came and took my baby daddy from right up under me.

Looking down at myself in one of Tremaine's plain white tee shirts, no bra, with a little bitty thong on underneath, I decided to go right ahead and work the Chyna magic on his ass before our son woke up. Grabbing up a plate, I placed four buttermilk pancakes on there, poured syrup and added a healthy portion of bacon and eggs, and made my way over to where he sat.

Standing directly in front of him, making sure my tee shirt was

47

purposely hiked high enough to expose my thighs, I looked down at him with that stupid phone in his hand, as he tapped on the screen looking as if he was sending a message. Trying my best not to suck my teeth in annoyance at him, I smiled and held the plate out to him.

"I made us some breakfast; I hope this is still your favorite." I put on a voice that was sexy but not too much. He looked up at me, almost as if he was trying not to scowl at my presence.

"I don't fuck with all that no more," he said with a blank, bored look on his face, his head tilted to one side a bit. I looked at him in confusion, because if I knew anything, was that Tremaine loved his stomach.

"What you mean Tre? You always loved a big, hearty breakfast." I shifted from one foot to the next, forgetting I was supposed to be acting sexy.

"Just what I said, I don't fuck with all that no more. I just normally eat a bowl of Trix cereal." Rocking back in his seat, he folded his arms across his bare chest and looked up at me totally expressionless.

Deciding right then and there I had enough of him and his childish ways, I sat down next to him, placing the plate on the floor.

"Tremaine, why are you being like this?" I sat fiddling with my fingers, my head bent in fake sorrow. "I know I was wrong for leaving with our son, but can't you see I'm trying to make it up to you?" I hesitated at first, but I eventually reached for his hand, and when he didn't pull away and allowed me to caress the inside of his palm with my fingertips, I smiled to myself.

"Please, can't you find it in your heart to somehow forgive me?"

I looked up at him shyly, and batted my fake, mink eyelashes at him. I saw his gaze slowly travel up my exposed thighs, drinking me in greedily with his eyes.

BINGO! I had him right where I wanted him. Leaning into him slowly, running my fingertips against his firm muscled chest, I made my way under his chin, forcing him to face me. I flicked my tongue, wetting my upper and then my lower lip, as I leaned in to kiss him.

Just as our faces were mere inches from each other's, I heard him say, "You must really think this is some kind of game, huh Chyna?" he said as he smirked at me, shaking his head. "You think I could forgive your lying, cheating ass just like that, after you took my son and left to go live with some random nigga? You think making me some shitty-ass pancakes gon' erase all the years I wondered where the fuck my son was at?" So this didn't go as I expected; Tremaine was mad! Fucking vein bulging in his neck and everything. I blame that stupid bitch— what was her name again? Aveeno? Bitch…

"How many times do you want me to say I'm sorry Tremaine, like damn…get over it already." I pulled back from him and rolled my eyes.

"Get over it?! Bitch, you lucky I don't hit females. Just so you know, as soon as you get a place to stay, I want you to get the fuck up out my crib. If it wasn't for my son, I would have kicked your ass out last night!" Shoving me away from him roughly, I was about to go the fuck off on him when his phone rang. Looking at the screen, his stupid face lit up like the fourth of July. He swiped the screen and stood up as he answered.

"Avi, I've been going crazy calling you." Really? This bitch again?

I didn't like this…I didn't like this one bit.

"What you mean we have nothing to talk about? Look, where you at? I'm coming to meet you, aight." With my eyes wide, I watched as Tremaine's sprung, punk ass all but ran in the direction of his bedroom. My blood ran like fire through my veins; I was livid! Who the fuck is this bitch? From what I saw earlier, she wasn't any type of competition compared to me.

I mean, what type of female wears dreads anyways? She may be a lesbian for all I know. Her clothes weren't even brand named, looked like she shopped at a garage sale. And you're telling me right now, that this was the person that had Tremaine tripping over his own two feet! The fuck… I must have stepped into the mothafuckin' Twilight Zone!

I sat and watched, unable to say anything as Tremaine came out, throwing a T-shirt over his head, his car keys in hand.

"When I get back I'll take little man out to get some ice cream or something, so I could get to know my son. Then me and you gonna figure out what's our next step with taking care of him and finding you guys a place to live. I'll be back." Without waiting for me to reply, he half walked, half jogged out the front door.

My chest heaved heavily as I sat on that sofa; I kept clenching my fists in and out. Oh! This Avion chick had no idea who she was up against, trying to come in and steal my man! Na, that bitch had another think coming.

She about to feel the wrath that is Chyna!

CHAPTER TEN

Avion

Coming Back To Get You!

I sat on the park bench and groaned loudly to myself, as I looked at the phone in my hand. Why did I do something so stupid as to call back Tremaine? But I guess curiosity got the best of me and made me dial his number. I sighed softly and looked on as the kids played happily, oblivious to all the turmoil that was taking place around.

I had my kids along with Dedra's; she needed a little free time dealing with Dornell's case, so she asked me to take the kids, so she could talk privately with her lawyer. I didn't mind, so I got my kids and brought everyone to run around in the park.

I looked up as the children screamed in excitement as they went up and down the slides, not a care in the world, and I smiled to myself. It was only then I noticed a woman was sitting next to me; I took her in from out the corner of my eye. She was attractive enough: she had pretty, dark skin, her hair hung in a ponytail. I could tell she had body by the way her hips were spread out on the bench she shared with me.

Going back to my thoughts about Tremaine, I honestly didn't quite know what should be done about him. I knew how these baby momma stories went; most times those women just didn't know how to let go. I was in no way about to get into it with another female for Tremaine. Besides, I saw Chyna, and she seemed a little out of my league. She had those expensive type bundles in her hair and a pretty, flawless face. She looked like the type of clothes she wore were nothing but designer. I definitely couldn't keep up with that!

However, there was a way I could afford to indulge in things that I only dreamed about…That was being down with this plan that Stormy devised. I had no choice but to put my big panties on, suck it up and at least hear exactly how we were going to accomplish this act. I hated to admit it to myself, but I desperately needed to do something about my finances; my kids needed to be with their mother.

As much as I hated to admit it to myself, I was actually giving being a part of a plan to commit a robbery some serious thought. What the fuck was wrong with me?!!

"Those your kids?" a voice next to me questioned softly. I turned to face the young woman who shared the park bench with me; she had kind eyes, and I smiled at her.

"Yes, only two though. You see that little girl with the pigtails and pink track suit on?" I said as I pointed out my kids to her. "And you see that other one that's making sure nobody pushes her little sister down? That's my older pooh bear." I knew I sounded like a mama bear, but I loved my kids so much.

"They are so pretty. The youngest don't look like you so much;

she must look like her daddy huh?" The stranger asked as her eyes focused on the playing foursome. My mind drifted to Jamal just then, because she was right—my youngest did look exactly like her father.

"Yes, she does look like her father," I said softly, my eyes drifting in the opposite direction of the kids. Just then my phone rang again. Looking at the screen, I saw it was Tremaine again, and I sighed heavily before answering.

"Where you at Avi?" he asked as I answered the phone. I looked up and scanned the playground.

"I'm sitting over at the slides Tremaine. I don't even know why you're wasting your time anyway. We have nothing to talk about." Sucking his teeth ever so rudely at what I just said, he hung up the phone on me.

Looking up again to see what the kids were up to, my eyes darted over to where they were last and there was no sign of them. Creasing my forehead, trying not to go in full panic mode, I took my time, letting my eyes roam slower this time over the playground…nothing.

"What in the hell," I said out loud as I stood up, my chest tight as fuck. I was beginning to feel as if I was having some sort of anxiety attack.

Turning around to the strange lady who was sitting next to me on the bench to ask her if she saw where my kids ran off to, I got the shock of my life when I realized that the spot she was sitting on was now empty. The fuck is going on? Am I being pranked?

"Misty!" I yelled out my eldest's name into the noisy playground of screaming, shouting, loud ass kids. My head was spinning from left to right, front to back looking desperately for the kids. Can you imagine my ass going back to Dedra's apartment telling her I lost her kids! I better just kill myself right now dammit!

"Misty! Shyann!...Shit" I ran off in the direction I saw them at last and bumped straight into a hard frame.

"The fuck is wrong with you Avi?" Tremaine's deep voice said against my ear, as I tried pulling away from him.

"The kids...the kids are gone." I was trying my best not to lose my cool, because maybe they were right here and it's just that my eyes haven't laid sight of them just yet.

"What! What you mean the kids are gone Avi?" He turned around scanning the park, never mind he had not a fucking clue what they looked like.

"I mean they are fucking gone Tremaine! I was sitting here talking to some random bitch...wait a minute." I back tracked in my mind at the strange lady that was sitting next to me asking questions. She disappeared the same time I noticed the kids were gone. Was she the one that took them?

"Oh my god!" I was fighting to regulate my breathing at the realization that the kids may have been kidnapped.

"Oh my god what Avion? What the fuck is going on?" Looking at Tremaine, feeling to be on the brink of tears, I was about to tell him about the strange woman when I heard familiar voices.

"Hi mommy!" With wide eyes I turned to the voice, and exhaled a breath of relief as all four kids came running up to where Tremaine and I stood, ice cream cones in hand, big smiles on all of their faces.

Racing over to them, not sure if to hug them or whoop their little asses, I stopped and dropped to my knees as they reached me and grabbed a hold of my youngest, pulling her into a tight embrace.

"Misty, where in the hell did you all run off to? You know better than to leave and not let me know where you are going." I scolded the eldest of my daughters as she licked on her ice cream cone with not a care in the world.

"And where in the hell did all four of you get those ice cream cones?" I said as I attempted to stop all of them from licking their cones, just as Tremaine came and stood next to us.

"Daddy gave it to us mommy." Shyann smiled up at me happily, her front tooth missing as she continued to devour her cone.

My jaw dropped open; that was the only reaction I could have done as Shyann's words tried their best to register in my head.

"Wh---what did you just say?" I whispered in disbelief as I stood to my feet, staring down at my daughters.

"Daddy bought all of us ice cream. Mommy you have a silly look on your face." Shyann giggled, as my mouth remained open, and my eyes were wide.

"And where did you see your daddy princess?" Tremaine asked as he bent down towards the girls, his hands on his knees.

"Who are you?" Misty asked rudely, as her eyes traveled over Tremaine, taking him in from head to toe.

"I'm a friend of your mommy. So tell me, where did you see your daddy?" I listened as Tremaine questioned my girls as my eyes darted around the park, desperately searching the grounds for any signs of Jamal.

"He was right over there by that big tree." All four of them spoke at the same time as they pointed towards a big, tall tree. Both Tremaine and myself made eye contact before our gaze fell on the tree.

"He was with his friend…a lady," Misty said with slight attitude.

"What she look like baby?" I said as I gently laid my hand in her hair, coaxing her to continue talking. I listened carefully as Misty described the stranger who sat next to me less than a half hour ago. So Jamal had this woman come distract me while he almost took off with my kids.

"Yes mommy, he told me to give you a message," Shyann said as she licked the ice cream that was now melting, and running down her hand.

"What's that Shyann?"

"He said to tell you he's coming back to get you real soon."

"Mothafucka," I heard Tremaine growl under his breath as he took off running in the direction of where the kids said Jamal was. Me on the other hand, I was too stunned to move, too scared to even breathe.

What the fuck does he mean he was coming back to get me real soon?

CHAPTER ELEVEN

Stormy

This Is What We About To Do!

I closed the door of my apartment as Avion and Dedra walked in. They both sat on my sofa like two robots, barely saying anything, and I knew something was up with them both.

"What the fuck is wrong with you two?" I walked to where they both sat and stood in front of them, looking as if they had the weight of the world on their shoulders. They both looked at each other, then to me; still saying nothing.

"You want to go first?" Dedra said to Avion, who exhaled loudly in frustration. Rolling my eyes to the heavens, I sat in the chair opposite them, because I knew this was about to be some bullshit.

"Well…..first off, Jamal isn't missing or dead. His dumb ass seems to be stalking me or some shit." Wait, what? I sat looking at Avion dumbfounded. Jamal is stalking her?

"Bitch…explain this shit." I began rubbing my temples, because I swear us three have to be the most unlucky bitches in Brooklyn!

I listened attentively as Avion rambled on about a trip to the park, some random heffa talking to her, the kids saying they saw their good-for-nothing daddy, and something about ice cream cones.

"The fuck does he mean he's coming back to get you real soon?" I was upset as a mothafucker. I felt like this was my husband acting the fool.

"Aye Dedra, if that motherfucker so much as comes within an inch of Avion, we….gon'…beat…his…ass!" I clapped dramatically after every word. Fuck Jamal's abusive ass; he gone get dealt with by two very aggressive females!

"You know this Stormy," Dedra said as she got up, and we gave each other high-fives. "We got you boo; we gon' take Jamal's ghost before we let that nigga lay a hand on you again," Dedra said as she gave Avion a reassuring hug, as Avi faked a weak smile.

"Ok, you next. What the fuck is wrong with you?" I turned my attention Dedra to see what her issue was. The last thing I needed was for these two not to have their minds right; everybody needed to be focused.

"Girl, you know how I told you Benjamin was coming over yesterday right?" I slapped my hand up to my forehead; I know this bitch didn't!

"Bitch! Don't tell me your ho ass done slept with your baby daddy's lawyer."

"Shut the fuck up Stormy. Ain't nobody finna fuck Benjamin." She was waving her hands around like she was tryna get buck.

"Ok well good; then what the fuck happened?" I listened in

nothing but pure amusement as she re-told her story of Dornell coming to his crib and finding another nigga there.

"Bitch! Oh my god!" I was hollering laughing as she said she had to literally pry Dornell's fingers from around Benjamin's neck. I never met the dude, but from what I heard so far from Dedra, her baby daddy was a silent lunatic; she definitely could not slip around him.

"Oh my god! Dedra what happened next? Did Dornell whoop your ass too?" I swear I don't even know why I found this so hilarious, but my black ass couldn't stop laughing at her demise.

"Dornell's drama queen ass turned and left the apartment, talking 'bout...he needed to leave before he killed my ass." I fell to the floor just then. I swear I was so stupid for this, but I couldn't stop laughing.

"That's what your ass get, bringing Benjamin in that man's apartment. You knew your horny ass was about to fuck that man." I wiped away the water from out my eyes, as I got up and took my spot back on the chair.

"Shut up Stormy. Let's get on to what we came here for in the first place," she said as she reached over and started playing with Avion's dreads. Getting myself together, I cleared my throat loudly.

"Na, but on the real, we'll keep an eye out for fuck boy Jamal, and don't worry Dedra...your man will be back home after he blows off some steam." Clapping my hands loudly I said to them, "Now! Let's get down to business."

"Ok, so I've been thinking really hard about this, and this is what we about to do. Y'all know what the next two weeks is right?" Both Dedra and Avion looked at each other confused.

"The beginning of Summer?" *This dense bitch*, I thought to myself as I scrunched my face up at Avion.

"I swear sometimes Avi…NO! The next two weeks will be the ending of the month, and the ending of the month is when Richard clears out his vault and makes the deposit to his bank. So this is when this has to happen." Nobody decided to say anything or ask any questions, so I continued.

"We have to be quick, and we have to be organized…" Before I could finish my sentence properly, Avion sprang up from her seat.

"We! Hold up Stormy, what you mean we? We are the ones about to rob Richard?" I was honestly beginning to think Jamal had knocked a few screws slack with all the beatings he gave Avion.

"So who you thought was about to do it Avi? Yes we." Her head started shaking from side to side violently. This bitch right here, I thought to myself as I looked at Avion acting like a straight scaredy cat.

"I don't think you two really even know what the fuck y'all really about to do." Avion began pacing floor as she looked at both me and Dedra. I decided to shut up and let her air her concerns in the open; and then I would decide if I would even bother including her in what I had planned. The last thing I wanted was someone who didn't have enough backbone to be a part of this.

I mean, yeah all of us are dealing with some shit right now that money definitely would fix, but let's face it—we aren't robbers. Looking as she threw her hands up in the air, right then and there I realized why she was getting her ass beat all these years from Jamal…she was weak! Plain and simple; but that's what good friends were for. I'm about to toughen this bitch the fuck up!

"Come here Avion, and sit down; let me explain how we gon' do this shit. And how we gon' get away with it." I smiled wide at her as she reluctantly walked back to her seat and sat down, folding her arms as she continued to look at me.

Standing before them, I began to explain my plan. "First off, it's not just gonna be us. We'll have to get a driver to get us out there the fastest way he can. Unless one of you bitches think you have what it takes to be a getaway driver?" I waited until they both shook their heads.

"That's what I thought. Secondly, I have somebody on the inside working with me."

"Hold up, what you mean you got somebody on the inside?" Dedra interrupted me, and I turned my attention to her and rolled my eyes.

"Well if you would let a bitch finish Dedra... this person knows Richard's office well, so they have already let me know exactly where that big ass vault is holding all his precious money. We have to be quick; we can't afford any slip ups, because the armored truck would be there on that exact day for the money pick up. And armored truck means security guards, and security guards mean loaded weapons. We're not trying to get shot doing this shit."

"Shot! Oh my god...this is too much." Avion was beginning to get on my last nerves. I took a deep breath and closed my eyes for a couple of seconds before I addressed her.

"Avi, relax... we are not about to go up in there without being strapped. I signed us up for a couple of classes in the shooting range. A friend hooked me up so we won't have to pay. Avion, don't worry, we can do this; have faith in yourself. Don't you want your kids back? I know you do." I bent down in front of her as I took hold of her hands she had clasped on her lap. She looked at me, and I smiled at her reassuringly.

"We got this boo; we can do this." And then slowly but surely, she smiled back at me and shook her head. YES! I cheered inside my head silently; this was step one of my plan.

"I got some questions Stormy," Dedra spoke up, and I focused my attention to her as I got up and walked over to the other sofa, taking a seat.

"Let me hear them."

"OK, so like do you have anybody in mind for the getaway driver? 'Cause I know a nigga a couple blocks from where we live. His nickname is Gas; that nigga could be in the next installment of *The Fast and the Furious*." I listened skeptically at Dedra.

"Dedra, but can you trust him? The last thing we need is a nigga that can't be trusted. Fuck around and end up with a bullet in our brain and all our money gone." I wanted to make sure we weren't dealing with no shady motherfuckers. The inside person I had was legit; I was sure of it.

"Yeah that nigga cool as fuck. I'll feel him out just in case though. So how we gonna do this? We can't just roll up in there and announce a stick up, so what's the plan?" I pounced up out of my seat in excitement, clapping my hands together as I made my way to my bedroom to where a box was. I grabbed up one of the articles of clothing and made my way back to Avion and Dedra.

I tossed the jumpsuit at Dedra. "When we run up in there this is what we'll be wearing." I sat back and watched as Dedra unfolded the jumpsuit, looking all types of confused.

"The fuck is this Stormy? Is this a janitor's outfit?" I laughed a little at the way Avion's face was twisted in confusion.

"Yes, it's a janitor's outfit. My inside guy got those for me. So on the day the regular cleaners will be getting a call saying they are not needed, and that's where we come in." When I say I've replayed this over and over in my head about how this needed to happen, I just know we could pull it off.

"This shit is crazy. So we'll have guns and everything?" I looked at Avion who wore a look as if she was about to pass out or some shit.

"Yes Avion, we'll have guns; hence the reason why I said we had shooting practice."

"Nobody will get hurt right Stormy? I just want to be sure we just gon' take the money and leave, and nobody will be hurt." Avion was such a scary bitch, I swear. I exhaled softly.

"I promise you nobody will get hurt." Of course that was bullshit. I had no way of knowing if anybody would get hurt or not. If someone did though, I'll be damned if it was gonna be one of us.

"Oh yeah, Avion…you're in charge of getting our masks. Dedra and I will handle everything else." I smiled as Avion shook her head in agreement somewhat reluctantly.

"Two weeks from now, we three about to become hood rich!"

CHAPTER TWELVE

Jamal

Old Acquaintances

"I bet she almost shit her pants when the kids told her they saw me." I chuckled softly under my breath as I got out the shower, drying myself with a towel, making sure to pay special attention to my bruised ribs.

Realizing that my words were met with silence, I walked slowly into the bedroom and looked over at Halo as she sat quietly, removing her shoes from off her feet.

"What's wrong with you?" I asked as I pulled the top drawer open, taking a plain white tee out.

"Nothing, she just seemed…kinda nice as I sat there talking to her." I stood in the middle of the bedroom, my eyes never leaving her as I finished getting dressed. Making my way over to where she sat, I stood before her and she began to cower back.

"What? You think I'm wrong for what I'm about to do? What the fuck were you two talking about anyway? I just asked you to distract her as I got the kids to come with me. Now it seemed as if you fell in love with her or some shit." Let me give y'all a brief introduction to this female that sat before me, with her eyes wide in fear with the thought that she was probably gonna get a good ass whopping.

I met Halo a couple years back, or maybe it was more than that, but who's counting. She was on her way to get her niece from school, the same school my kids attend, and I swear it was nothing but pure faith that the only day I decided to pick my kids up, I met her. She was looking sexy as hell in her little mini denim dress, hips rocking from left to right, her thighs thick and nice like how I preferred them. I pulled up on her ass, spit my game, and as the saying goes, the rest was history!

"We were just talking about the kids Jamal; I promise you that was it." I grimaced down at her as I made a fist, and smiled inwardly when she placed her hand up to her face. But really and truly, I was just fucking with her.

"Good! I hope for your sake that was all you spoke about." I turned and moved away from her just as I heard a loud knocking at the door.

"Go let my nigga in real quick," I said to her. She wasted no time springing to her feet to answer the door to let my cousin Craig in. Trailing behind slowly as she made her way to the front door, I smiled wide as he walked through the door.

"My nigguh! What's up man? How are you healing?" We gave each other daps and made our way across to the chocolate colored sectional that I bought, might I add; and we took a seat next to each other as Halo got out of the room to give us our privacy.

"I was beginning to wonder what the fuck was up with you man. Went by your crib and it looked like it was deserted and shit." I passed my hands swiftly through my hair as I listened to Craig. After that stupid nigga beat my ass, I decided to lay low and not let anybody know exactly where I was. Me and my cousin had always been tight, so I decided to let him know where I had been at all this time, telling him very little about my encounter with an old acquaintance of the both of us.

"Yo' me and Avion separated my nigga." I turned to him as his face lit up in shock at what I just admitted.

"Say word Jamal? You two are separated? Did she find out about shawty you been kicking it with?" he asked, speaking about Halo. Of course he knew about her, I just never mentioned to many details, like where she lived and all that. Craig was my cousin and all, but don't get shit twisted; he was the type of nigga you never left your girl around. This nigga will most definitely snatch her from right up under you! Exactly what happened with him and Avion, but we'll get to that in a minute.

"Hell naw! She didn't find out about Halo. Come to find out this sneaky bitch been fucking another dude right up under my nose the whole time." Craig whistled softly, as he shook his head at me.

"Aye, I done told you about Avion. She's no good...always was my nigga; I tried to warn you." I shook my head in agreement because he did try to warn me. You see about a month after Avion and I were married, Craig and I went out to have a couple beers. Back then I was head over heels in love with Avion, even though I liked my women thick and curvy; it didn't even bother me much that Avion was more on the slim side with her light brown dread locks. I loved every inch of that woman, that is until Craig confessed something to me that night that changed my life for good.

"I know, and I should have listened to you from that night when you told me she let you hit it; just can't trust females man." Yeah you guys read correct, that slut of a wife I had let my cousin, my own blood, fuck her nasty ass. You see, my cousin and I had this thing we always did; if one of us liked a chick, we would let the other one pretend that he's interested in her just to see what type of female we tryna get with.

So, Craig actually was the one who came up with the plan to put Avion to the test; he said he had a feeling about her. But I insisted she was one of the good ones, no need to test her, but he kept telling me I shouldn't be too quick to put all my trust in her; so I gave in to his demands. And imagine my surprise when a month after we got married he came and said he was successful, and that he slept with my wife…MY wife!

So, guess what I decided to do? That's right, I made her ass pay. I never told her I found out about what she did with Craig. Na, that would be way too easy; so instead I did a full 360 on her ass. It was like I turned into Mr. Hyde. I went from being the nice, caring, thoughtful husband and father, to being a raging and abusive lunatic.

With every slap, punch and kick that I gave to Avion throughout the years, it was all for fucking with my cousin. But anyway…moving on from all that, let's deal with the matter at hand.

"But guess what nigga? You'd never believe who's the dude she is cheating on me with. You gon' crack up." I chuckled as I shoved his arm, waiting for his reply. His face had a total blank look on it. Besides he would have never figured it out anyway, so I went ahead and told him.

"Remember that house we robbed a while back, ran up in there and stole all their drugs and money and shit?" Craig's gaze drifted off for a few seconds, as he tried to remember exactly what I was talking about. Snapping his fingers he looked over at me, broad grin on his lips.

"Oh yeah! That's when we had to smoke that loud mouth nigga who didn't wanna do what he was told." Craig ran his fingers across his full beard that he took so much pride in. My cousin was far from a handsome nigga. He was a nutmeg colored nigga with a bald head and more on the heavy side, but he was a smooth talker; talked his way straight into those bitch's panties. He had a huge scar on his neck, given to him by his friend....well his so-called friend, after he tried to slit his throat when Craig was just seventeen years old. My cousin came home after collecting a large sum of money from one of the niggas he had selling dope for him one night. Soon as he walked into his apartment that little dumb nigga was waiting on him, didn't ask a goddamn question. Just ran his knife right into Craig's neck. As he was busy taking the money, Craig opened his eyes and saw it was his very own friend that tried to end his life over a few hundreds.

Long story short, Cali...Craig's homeboy, was never seen or heard from again after Craig came out of the hospital; that fool got dealt with.

Moving on…

"Na nigga, you smoked that fool, not me." I laughed as I pointed my fingers at him.

"Anyway, his brother he was with that night, that's the same nigga Avion fucking around on me with," I said as I repeatedly tapped Craig's arm, as he looked at me with wide eyes.

"Say word? wait a minute…how you know that though? You seen them together or something?" Craig asked, so I proceeded to tell him the long story about him showing up at my work, beating my ass, and telling me to stay away from my own fucking wife.

"You know where that nigga stay at man?" Craig was up on his feet in a heartbeat. This nigga was a savage to his heart for real; any reason to get buck and he was ready for it.

"Yeah, Avion led me to where he lives the other morning; I've been watching and following her ass from a distance, just waiting for the right time to snatch her dumb ass up." I stood up along with him, as we were now facing each other, mean mug on each of our faces.

"Just say the word when you wanna do this. Been a while since I've bust my gun; *rahhh-rahhh-rahhhh*!" Craig made the action as if he was firing a machine gun, and I laughed, because if anybody I knew had my back was this nigga right here.

"Soon nigga, real soon; we gonna snatch both their asses up and handle that!"

CHAPTER THIRTEEN

Tremaine

Aveeno... Avion!

You know a roach is one of the hardest things to get rid of right? Well, I was beginning to think that Chyna was half roach, half human! Couldn't shake this trick for nothing. It's been five whole days since she showed up at my apartment with my son, and her ass still here! *The only positive out of all this was my son,* I thought to myself as I turned to look at him.

He slowly started to come around, and now he was comfortable enough with me to sit with me and play video games. We both were sprawled out on the floor of my condo as we battled each other in *Grand Theft Auto V.* His mother was somewhere in the condo doing whatever the hell she does all day. Her ass better be looking for a damn job and a place to stay.

"So, am I 'post to call you daddy?" My little man was so cute. The way he always looked up at me with those big brown eyes melted the old thug in me almost instantly.

"Yes lil' man, you can call me daddy. Matter of fact, I would love it if you call me daddy." I smiled at him, and he smiled right back, and right then and there I felt the need to get up from off that floor, walk up to Chyna, and headbutt her ass. Had me missing out on my son's life with her selfish bullshit.

"OK....daddy!" He giggled after his first use of the word.

"Come on baby; let's get you in the shower alright. You'll finish your video games after you're done with your bath." I snickered a little as Trevelle continued laying there, full concentration on his face as he pressed the keys on the control like crazy, as he continued to ignore his mother.

"Aye, don't you hear me talking to you?" Catching me completely off guard, Chyna bent snatching my son roughly up by his upper arm as if he was a grown man.

"Ouch mummy," Trevelle whimpered out in pain, as he was dragged to a standing position.

My paternal instincts wasted no time in kicking in. Dashing the control to the ground, I quickly placed my hand on Chyna's shoulder, pushing her away from my son. Before I knew what I was doing, I was down in her face going the fuck off.

"Don't you ever lay your hands on my son like that, as if he's a grown man. The fuck is wrong with you.?" My chest was rising and falling with rage as I stared at her. Looking down at my son whose eyes began welling up with tears, I bent to talk to him.

"Aye, look at daddy." Slowly his eyes traveled up until they met mine.

"Us Taylor men don't cry aight." He shook his head slightly at me. "And I promise you this is the last time your momma will ever talk to you and man handle you like that, alright." He looked over to his mother, as if he was looking for some kind of reassurance from her, but I put my hand under his chin and turned his head to me.

"You don't be scared of her. I'm your daddy, and I'll always be here to protect you. Ya heard me!" Smiling shyly, he shook his head at me.

"Aight lil' man, you go on in and have a shower, and when you done I'll go take you for some ice cream ok?" That instantly brought a huge smile to his face, and he ran off quickly in the direction of the bathroom. As I got up, I turned to Chyna, who saw the anger in my face and stumbled two steps backwards as I charged towards her, grabbing her by her upper arms and pinning her against the wall.

With my index finger less than an inch away from her face, I clenched my jaw tightly as I spoke to her, "Let this be the first, and last time, I ever see you handle my seed like that. The fuck is wrong with you, he's just a baby; you treating him as if he's a grown ass man." Chyna only managed to ignite my anger with her fake ass water works she knew how to turn on so well.

"I didn't mean any harm to him Tremaine." She sniffled as she tried to caress my face, but I tilted my head to the side so she wouldn't be able to touch me.

"Why are you treating me like this Tremaine, is it because of that Aveeno bitch?" And just like that, all of her fake crying came to an abrupt halt, with her pretending ass.

"First off, don't call my lady no goddamn bitch!" Her eyes narrowed angrily when I said the word lady.

"Secondly, her name is Avion." I liked the way Chyna's nose began to flare in anger; I was enjoying this way more than I should.

"And thirdly, the only person to be blamed for the treatment you're receiving from me… is YOU! Stop blaming other people when you know damn well all this is on you Chyna." I relaxed the grip I had on her arm when I saw that for the first time, what I said actually got to her, as she bent her head thoughtfully before making eye contact once again with me.

As she looked up at me, and I swear I can't make this up if I tried, she reached for my face and with no warning whatsoever, she slammed her mouth against mine. Pushing her tongue against my mouth as she forced its way in, she dragged her tongue playfully with mine as they entwined with each other. So I bet you all are wondering why I didn't immediately push her off of me, right?

Well…before I'm anything, I'm a man; and that shit she was doing with her tongue, plus the way she was moaning so seductively into my mouth as she rubbed herself slowly on my body that was responding to her on its own free will… a nigga ain't gonna lie, shit felt good as fuck; almost made a nigga want to hit…..ALMOST!

Taking my hands and placing them on her chest, I gently but firmly pushed her into the wall behind her.

"The fuck off me Chyna. What you think this is shawty, fuck with Tremaine day?" I asked her as I backed away from her. She looked somewhat stunned that her advances that she made to me didn't work.

"We not about to do this right now. You left Chyna…you, not me. I don't even want you like that." With my hands up facing her, I waved them left to right to add emphasis to my words.

"That's not what it felt like to me Tremaine. That anaconda was ready to come out and play." She smiled like the little she devil she was as she licked her lips; her eyes never left mine.

"Think I give a fuck about that bitch, she's not even on my level. She don't have me shook. All you need is a little more time, and you'll be mine again." *This bitch done lost her mind*, I thought as I stared at her in a daze.

"Aye, don't make me kick your psycho ass out my shit. Avion is who I want…and who I'm going to be with; so your crazy ass can kick bricks. Now hurry up and go attend to my son and let me take him for some Haagen-Daz." Throwing her head back, she laughed like I just told the funniest joke of all time.

"We'll see about that Tremaine," were her parting words as she turned and made her way to the direction of the bathroom.

Ok! So it was obvious that I had to get Chyna the fuck up out my condo. Starting tomorrow, I was definitely about to start searching for an apartment for her.….shit, a nigga would even pay the first couple months rent for her; anything just to get her out of here. From what I saw, I needed to take my son away from her also, because if I find out she's been abusing Trevelle, Jesus would need to be taking a whole lot more than just the wheel where she's concerned.

CHAPTER FOURTEEN

Dedra

Shoot 'Em Up!

"*If* you don't bring your drama queen ass home tonight, I'm through with your ass Dornell! Fuck you think this is?" Sucking my teeth loudly, I ended the call and got out the car along with Avion and crazy mothafucking Stormy. Don't even know how she even managed to talk me into this bullshit.

But on the other hand, I was glad my blood wasn't as thin as Avion's, because I still haven't been able to find a job. And Dornell's boss told him he'd call him as soon as more deliveries came through. Of course I don't believe he had any plans on calling him back to work. So in a nutshell, my life was in the toilet!

I desperately needed a miracle to happen to set me back on the right track, and this miracle was about to happen in the next week.

Before I get to all that, let me talk about this fairy I had for a baby daddy! Well since the day he and Benjamin went at it like Mike Tyson and Muhammad Ali, and he beat the shit out of Benjamin—I'm talking about straight up almost killed him—anyway, Dornell came home later on that night, packed up a few of his clothes, and gave me the deuces sign; informing me he'd be staying over at his mom's place for a while. Big baby!

That was about a week ago, and this nigga still bitchin'! Every day I'm practically begging his stupid ass to come on home, reciting to him over and over that absolutely nothing happened between Benjamin and I. But he just was not hearing it. Now mind you, a bitch hasn't gotten no dick since forever; I'm irritable as fuck and Dornell's been playing with my emotions since he got out. Should have really fucked Benjamin, since I'm being accused of it almost every goddamn day.

"Would you two hurry up! Damn, a bitch don't got all day," I shouted back at Avion and Stormy, as I led the way into the building where we were about to have our first, and only, shooting practice.

"What's wrong with Dedra?" I heard Avion whisper behind me to Stormy, as if I couldn't hear her or something.

"What's wrong with Dedra," Stormy replied as loud as she could, making sure that I could hear her, "is that she needs that vitamin D, and not the kind you can get over the counter in a pharmacy." As she chuckled with her dumb self at the mess she just said, I turned to the back of me so I could look at Stormy, and rolled my eyes hard at her.

"Shut the fuck up Stormy. Just because Xavier been riding your back out almost every night, doesn't mean you get to make fun of the less fortunate." Both she and Avion laughed as we entered the building and made our way to the front desk.

"Aye, where PJ at?'" Stormy asked the short, dark-skinned girl who stood behind the counter.

"He's at the back," she said rudely. One would have sworn she wasn't getting paid to do her job by the disgruntled look she had on her face.

"Well go get him then. Tell him Stormy's here to see him." Popping her gum she was gnawing on like she was a damn goat, she rolled her eyes a little at Stormy before making her way through the back door.

"Un-mannerly bitch," Stormy muttered as she shook her head.

"Oh, listen up guys," I said in a hushed tone as I moved closer to the both of them. "I spoke to Gas yesterday; he said he's down. Just wants to know what his cut is going to be," I said as I looked over at Stormy.

"Dedra, are you sure we can trust this guy? I don't want any problems aight!" Stormy pointed her finger in my face as if she was scolding one of her kids. Sucking my teeth, I slapped her finger out of my face.

"Shut up Stormy, and move your goddamn finger from out of my face. Yes we can trust him. He's cool with both me and Dornell; known him for a minute now." I turned my neck left and right as I spoke. But all Stormy did was narrow her eyes at me skeptically.

"I'm just tryna—" That was all she was able to get out when a loud, booming voice shouted out to her.

"Well if it isn't the tropical Storm of my life!" *Well damn*, I thought to myself as I turned to face a guy who could be Reggie Bush's twin brother. Nice coffee complexion, low fade haircut, wonderful broad shoulders that held up a wide neck...and a full set of sexy lips. Jesus

Christ, Dornell needed to give me some, and quick!

"Hey there handsome." Avion and I stood to the side as Stormy and PJ greeted each other with a kiss, full on the lips too.

"When you gon' stop playing with a nigga's feelings and marry me Stormy?" *Well damn*, I thought to myself once again, because he actually did look quite sincere when he said that just then.

"You play too much," Stormy said as she playfully knocked him on his shoulder. "Come meet my girls real quick," she said as she took him by his hand, leading him over to us.

"These are my ride-or-dies: this is Avion, and this is my girl Dedra." Avion and I smiled at him, of course my gaze lingered on him a little too long. And of course Stormy had to be the one to notice.

"This one here hasn't been getting any dick in a while, you might wanna be careful around her; she might start dry humping your leg." I was absolutely mortified at what she just said, as both she and PJ laughed at my expense.

"Shut the fuck up Stormy! Thinking you cute," I scolded her as she continued laughing.

"She always says that," she said to PJ as she linked both her and PJ arms together and made her way in the direction of the door, from which he came.

"Come on ladies! Let's go shoot 'em up!"

So… plot twist! We've been here a little over a half hour now, shooting off these guns like crazy. And out of the three of us, guess who hit their mark every time; I'm saying every single time!

Yup! None other than Avion. She was a beast with that 9mm in her hand. Direct hit to the heart or head every time she fired her weapon.

"Well we know who our shooter gon' be, just in case shit pops off next weekend," Stormy said about an hour and a half after, as we made our way to the parking lot to my car.

"Where you learn to have perfect aim like that Avi?" I asked as I disabled the alarm to my car, tugging on the handle to get in.

"I dunno know Dedra. I have steady hands from all the hair I do; maybe it's from that," Avion said as she took the hair band out of her hair, letting her dread locks free as she sat in the car.

"Hey, none of that matters, so long as her aim is good on that day," Stormy said as she sat in the front seat. "By the way, did you get the masks Avi?"

Both Stormy and I focused our attention on Avion, who nodded her head as she bent to retrieve a bag that sat between her feet.

"Yeah, I did…check them out," she said as she handed Stormy a plain, black plastic bag. My nosey self was bobbing and weaving trying to see what she got. However, when Stormy took the mask out, both of us looked first at each other, then down to the mask once more, mouth gaping open.

"Really Avi?" Stormy exclaimed, as she turned around to face Avion, "Bitch! You had one fucking job, one job Avi. The fuck is this?" I couldn't help but crack a smile as Stormy held up the mask, her face contorted in disbelief. Y'all know the movie *Scream* right? Well, Avion done went out and bought the exact same ghost face mask!

"So, we about to run up in there, looking like the cast of a scary movie. Avi, I ought to bop you in your damn head." Stormy looked around in the back seat at Avion, who had a look on her face like she didn't know what was the problem.

"Well unless you wanted to run up in there looking like the Avengers...that was all that was left." So, I'm sitting there, my eyes darting from left to right, back and forth at them both; and couldn't hold it in any longer. I fell out laughing, like literally screaming my head off.

And just like that, all three of us were laughing, each of us with a mask in hand, hollering like a bunch of fools.

"Yo, Avi I swear bitch....you lucky we love your ass!" I said as I leaned in the back and hugged my girl tightly. "Don't worry, these will do fine Stormy, besides...it will hide Avion's dreads perfectly." Last thing we needed was for any distinguishing features we had to be visible.

Shaking her head, and looking at the mask, Stormy covered her face, placing the mask over her head. With the ghost face mask on she playfully yelled out to us, "What's upppp!"

Our mood was light and fun...for now. Less than a week from now we were about to get TURNT!

CHAPTER FIFTEEN

Dornell

The Guys

Well it's the original Alpha male here, your boy Dornell! And I know you guys probably think I should give my girl a second chance right? But naw, hell naw! She was foul for having that nigga up in my crib. If she didn't have to literally pry my fingers from off his neck, I would have fucked around and killed his ass. Probably make some kind of record for the only nigga to be released from prison and end right back in there in just a matter of hours.

After I was sitting up in that jail cell for some foul shit that Dedra done, you think she would be a little bit more loyal and honest than having that sleazy lawyer in my place. So right now my main focus is getting a job and making sure my kids are straight. So for now I've been over at my mom's place, who wasn't very pleased to have to accommodate her grown ass son, but I let her know that it was going to be temporary. But right now a nigga about to get a fresh new look, about to get rid of these cornrows and let the barber do his thing.

As I pushed open the door to the barber salon and walked in, I heard gasps and shouts.

"I've been hearing you were out my nigga!" A homeboy I knew from a couple blocks from where I lived got up from out his seat and gave me daps.

"What's up Gas? You good my nigga?" I sat down and waited for the barber, who was about to be done with someone's haircut. I think if I'm not mistaken this the homeboy Dedra told me about that her friend Stormy been kicking it with; think his name is Xavier. I knew him from seeing him around the way, but we never actually spoke.

"You know how I do; stay tryna get these pockets fatter," Gas stated as he chuckled a bit. I smiled along with him, but niggas like Gas was the type of niggas you had to stay clear away from if you were trying to stay on the straight and narrow. This nigga's criminal record was longer than the waiting line for the new iPhone! He had everything from attempted robbery, possession of guns and ammunition, possession of drugs, even attempted murder. You name it, this nigga done did it!

"Careful in what you do to get them pockets fatter. You don't wanna end up back in prison my nigga." He looked completely un-fazed by my words, and he shrugged it off. Shaking my head, I looked away from him at the barber who summoned to me as soon as the guy got up from off his seat.

"What you about to do today player?" the barber asked as I took a seat and looked at myself in the mirror, hair standing up on ends.

"I want this gone," I said as I pulled thoughtfully at my hair. "I wanna cut it all off." The barber smiled and rubbed his chin, as he was also sporting cornrows.

"I've been thinking 'bout doing just the same, so I feel you," he said, placing the barbering coat around my neck. Since he seemed like a cool dude, I decided to query my suspicions.

"Hey, I think your girl and my girl are friends." He stopped midway of turning on his barbering equipment to look at me quizzically.

"Who, Stormy?"

"Yeah, you Xavier right?" He shook his head in agreement at me, as he slowly passed the trimmer through my head, and hair fell softly onto my shoulders.

"My girl…well she not my girl no more, but her name is Dedra." His eyes lit up in recognition as we made eye contact in the mirror.

"Oh, word. You the cat that was in prison right? Dornell." *Well I see Dedra had our business in the streets as usual,* I thought to myself.

"Yeah, that's me alright." I got silent as I saw my hair get shorter and shorter, suddenly wondering if this was such a good idea or not.

"Yeah she told me what happened man, about you meeting that lawyer nigga in yo' crib and shit. But, she also said nothing happened between him and your girl." I snorted loudly in disagreement.

"You didn't see what I saw; she was all hugged up on him when I walked in. I almost killed him dead too." He snickered softly at my words.

"Naw dog, I think you should talk to her some more about it. Not my business or nothing, just seems to me, according to my nosey girlfriend, that she really misses you." I listened to his words, letting everything sink in; I had to go by the apartment after to get some clothes and stuff, maybe I'd talk to her then.

"I hear you, good looking out man." I sat and watched as Xavier did his thing. He was pretty good at his job I must say, as he trimmed and shaped my hair. We managed to hold a light conversation, him talking about his crazy girl Stormy and me talking about my just as crazy baby momma. Every so often my eyes would fall on Gas, who was deep in conversation on his phone with somebody, probably thinking of a scheme on how to rob some damn body I bet.

"That nigga always getting himself mixed up in some shit," I mumbled softly to myself, not meaning for Xavier to hear, but he did anyway.

"If that ain't the truth; let me tell you what I heard about him—" Before his sentence was completed, the door to the shop opened and in walked a brother I don't think I've ever seen before. He and Xavier seemed familiar though, as he said, "What's up X." Before taking a seat.

"Oh wait, hol'up; come here Tremaine." Xavier hollered and waved him over, causing him to get up and walk over to us.

"This Dedra's nigga... Dornell, Dornell meet Avion's new nigga... Tremaine. Fuck that lame Jamal." My eyes almost bugged out their damn sockets. Avion had a new nigga? I honestly didn't even think she had it in her to leave that stupid ass Jamal, but I'm glad she did; she deserved way better than him.

"Nice to meet you man; I guess we three have something in common huh!" All three of us snickered shaking our heads. Just then Gas got up and made his way out the door, phone still glued to his ear;

I just knew he was up to no good.

Whatever it was, I was just glad it affected me in no way at all. The street life was a life I gave up a long time ago before I even meet Dedra. Reason why I didn't associate myself with niggas like Gas, they would just suck you right back into that lifestyle.

"Speaking 'bout that nigga, let me holla at the both of you." My eyebrows creased in question at Xavier as he spoke; both me and Tremaine looked at him, preparing to hear about what he had to say.

CHAPTER SIXTEEN

Tremaine

My Girl

As I walked around my condo butt ass naked, yes I said butt ass naked! Chyna was no longer in my space. The only problem was just how much I missed my son, but I called him twice a day since they left three days ago. I got a nice little apartment for them out in New York. I was even kind enough to pay the rent for a full six months, telling Chyna her ass needed to get up and find a job to support herself. I would be keeping frequent checks to make sure that she does just that.

Moving on, back to my nakedness; I was preparing for a date with my girl...Avion. Since the other week ago when we realized that her stupid husband was back, and from the looks of things he was no doubt stalking her ass, I wanted nothing more than to protect her from any harm. I've been trying to get her to move in with me, so that I could have an eye on her at all times, but she kept saying she doesn't think Jamal will harm the mother of his kids.

Um... to me that was beyond stupid. That nigga almost killed her more than a month ago. What makes her think he won't hesitate to try his best to put her six feet under! I swear Avion had a severe case of battered wife syndrome; that nigga wrapped himself around her mind in the worst way.

But I had a surprise for her. You see, I knew just how much she loved hairdressing, so the other day I saw this nice little shop with a for sale sign in front, and I bought it for her. Let her do her own thing; make those coins on her own.

So as I made my way to my bedroom, monster swinging and slapping my thigh as I hurriedly got dressed to wait in anticipation for Avion, I reached for the keys to the newly purchased salon on top of my dresser, and I smiled. I know things had been pretty rough on her moving back and forth to Dedra's and then to her granny's cramped one bedroom apartment on some days. I believed if I offered to get her an apartment she would have looked at it as a handout. She was hard headed, so instead I got her the salon; that way she could earn her own living and be able to pay her own rent for an apartment. I was praying she wasn't about to fight me on this.

Throwing on a pair of burgundy sweat pants and a plain white tee, I made my way into the kitchen to check on the food I ordered. Because a nigga could burn in the kitchen, and I do mean that literally... I would burn that shit down. So I ordered some Thai food from a restaurant not too far away. I plated the food as I waited for Dedra to drop Avion off, since she insisted I shouldn't come get her.

Ten minutes after I was sitting, sipping on my beer, there was a light knock on the door. Man, I shot up out my seat so quickly I almost tripped over my own two feet. The way I felt about Avion was nothing close to what I thought I felt for Chyna…I made my way over to the door, pulling it open.

"Goddamn!" I exclaimed as I took in the sight of Avion as she stood shyly before me. She wore a pair of black, short denim distressed jeans, exposing her nice, slim, toned thighs and a baby pink spaghetti strapped top and a pair of black, low-cut Converse on her feet. Her dreads were in a nice up do and she had little to no make-up on, just the way I liked.

"I told Dedra these pants were way too short," she said softly as she tugged on the fabric, somewhat in annoyance.

Taking her by the hand, I led her inside, closing and locking the door behind us.

"Baby, you look so fine to me, just perfect. Come sit down with your man." She blushed like crazy at my words, as she allowed me to lead her over to my sofa. Fuck feeling hungry for Thai food, my mouth was salivating for the sweet taste of Avion. I licked my lips unconsciously at my thoughts.

"Why you looking at me all funny Tremaine?" This woman that sat before me had no idea just how fucking beautiful she was; and that to me was a damn shame.

"Because Avi, I'm suddenly not hungry for food; I wanna eat you," I whispered in her ear, as my lips brushed lightly against it. I heard her take a sharp intake of breath, and saw her pores visibly rise on her arm.

"You missed me as much as I missed you babe?" I asked as I

continued kissing and sucking on her earlobe, making my way to her lips that were already parted. She shook her head in agreement as she closed eyes. I loved the way she was responding to me; I almost forgot that I had a surprise for her. Kissing her softly on her lips, her tongue gently touched my lips, prying them open. We kissed hungrily for a couple seconds before I pulled away, knowing damn well I would have my way with her right here on this sofa, but later on for that; we had enough time.

"Come on, let's eat." I got up from off my seat and made my way to the food already plated, to give her one.

"You cooked Tre?" She smiled, raising her eyebrows and wiggling them at me in humor, because she knew damn well I didn't cook.

"Avi if I cooked all we would be having was a bowl of cereal." She laughed, closing her eyes as she did, and I enjoyed the way I was starting to notice little things about her, like the way her eyes creased at the corners when she smiled. Taking a seat next to her once more, we began eating, chatting mostly about her kids.

Roughly twenty minutes after having eaten all of our food, we were now sipping on some Hennessy as Avion had her foot on top of my lap, as I rubbed her pretty manicured feet every chance I got. I decided to ask something that had been weighing on my mind.

"Hey."

"Yeah?" she replied as she looked up at me with dazed eyes, because Henny would do that to you every time. I smiled as I thought about all the freaky things I would be doing to her later on tonight.

"You know you could tell me anything right," I asked as she

looked at me quizzically, exactly like I knew she would. I continued playing with her feet, making slow circles on the soles; if you touched the correct spot under one's feet, you could actually make a person orgasm! I kid you not.

"Yes I know. Why you ask?" She sipped slowly, her eyes staring at me over the rim of her glass. I shrugged my shoulders, looking down at her pretty feet in my hands.

"So…you have anything you wish to get off your chest?" I pried again, as I removed the glass from her lips and she narrowed her eyes at me, no doubt wondering where exactly I was coming from.

"What exactly are you getting at Tremaine?" She tilted her head with a little bit of attitude. Deciding to just drop the topic, I was about ready to tell her about the surprise: me buying her her very own hair salon.

"Forget all that; look I got a surprise for you." She smiled, and I started feeling a bit nervous because I didn't quite know how she would react. As I reached into my pocket for the keys, my cell phone began ringing beside me on the sofa. I sucked my teeth in annoyance, wondering who was it that had the worst timing as I picked up my phone. Chyna popped up on my screen and I shook my head; here we go, I thought as I answered.

"Tremaine!" Chyna shouted in my ear in full panic mode.

"What's wrong?" I asked her, feeling the hair on the back of my neck stand up, because I just had a feeling something was wrong with my son.

"It's Trevelle," she sputtered out between sobs.

"What's wrong with my son Chyna?" Avion quickly removed her feet from off my lap and sat upright, looking at me in concern.

"I think he fell; I think his arm is broken. Can you come take us to the hospital?" Not even putting much thought into it, I got up, racing about my condo looking for my car keys.

"Just hol'up alright, I'm on my way." Avion was now standing, her eyes following me around as I finally found my keys, my mind just all over the place worrying about my son. How the hell did he even fall? And where in the hell was Chyna when he fell? She's going to have to answer a lot of motherfuckin' questions when I get to her apartment.

"What's happening Tre? What happened to your son?" Avion asked softly at my side as she gently placed her hand on my shoulder.

"His careless mother said he fell and his arm may be broken." She gasped, putting her finger tips to her lips, her eyes wide.

"Wait here until I get back aight." I turned to Avion, bending to give her a quick kiss on her lips. "Besides I still have to tell you what the surprise is." She smiled weakly at me, and I gave her a quick reassuring hug.

"I hope he'll be ok."

"For his mother's sake, he better be!" Those were the last words I uttered before I bolted out the door, making my way to Chyna's apartment to see what happened to my son.

CHAPTER SEVENTEEN

Dedra

Finally!!

*S*o guess what? I finally got some dick y'all! I feel like my old self again. And yes, I got it from Dornell and not Benjamin. Let me give y'all the 411 on how it went down. It happened about three nights ago. I awoke to what sounded like someone in my apartment; laying silent for a minute, I thought it was Avion, but then I remembered she was staying over at her grandmother's house. So I almost shit in my Victoria's Secret underwear with the realization that some no good nigga had broken into my place, and that I had to protect myself and my kids on my own. Grabbing my phone to check on the time, I saw it was now one in the morning. Getting up as quietly as I could, trying my best to make as little noise as possible, I stood listening as I heard the sounds of footsteps moving around in the apartment. Trying my hardest not to panic, I began thinking of what I could use as some type of weapon.

Remembering Dornell had bought a baseball bat for reasons just like this one, I quickly raced over to the closet doors, grabbing up the heavy ass bat. Looking down at my appearance, I was clad only in my bra and underwear, but I didn't have time for being modest. I had to fuck this nigga up; let that motherfucker know he stepped into the wrong bitch's apartment.

Taking a deep breath, giving myself a reassuring pep talk in my mind, I walked towards the door and grabbed hold of the handle, opening it slowly. The corridor that led to the living room was dark as fuck as I cautiously made my way down the aisle, too scared to even breathe fearing that the thief would hear. As soon as I came to the end of the corridor and was about to turn into the living room, I bumped right into a hard body, almost knocking me to the ground.

Without thinking twice, I swung the bat straight at the silhouetted frame, hitting him straight in his torso.

"Ouch! Dedra what the fuck!"

What the hell, I thought to myself, dropping the bat at the sound of the familiar voice. Racing to the light switch, I flipped it on and my eyes opened wide with shock at the sight of Dornell doubled over in pain, holding his stomach.

"Dornell! What the hell you doing creeping through here in the dark like a damn roach!" I shouted, as I made my way over to him.

"Fuck, I came over to get a few more of my things," he grimaced, as he struggled to stand in an upright position. I held on to his upper arm, trying to assist him when I noticed he cut all of his cornrows off. In spite of me almost damn near bludgeoning my baby daddy to death, with his own baseball bat, I smiled at his new appearance because he looked fine as hell.

"Maybe you should have done this at a more suitable time rather than one in the morning Dornell." He placed his arm around my neck for support as I continued to help him as we made our way to the bedroom. I helped him to the bed and stood up, folding my arms under my breasts as I looked down at him, and shook my head as he continued rubbing his stomach. He looked up at me angrily, but it was his own fault for coming up in here unannounced.

"I just didn't want the kids to see me getting my stuff and leaving, that's all." My expression softened, and I moved in closer to him and caressed his newly faded haircut.

"This looks good; I like it. How's your stomach? You want a glass of water?" I asked, reaching down to gently massage his stomach as we looked at each other.

Taking a hold of my wrist, Dornell looked at me for like almost ten seconds before he asked the question, "You fucked that lawyer Dedra?" His face stone cold as he waited on my reply. Sucking my teeth softly, I pouted my lips out before answering, "I done told you a million times Dornell... No, I didn't!" We stared at each other for a while longer before I looked away in annoyance.

"You so stupid sometimes Dornell. Why would I go and fuck some lawyer after all that you did for me? You sat up in that jail cell for something I did, and that's how you think I'm gon' repay you? By fucking your lawyer? How could you even think that low of me? I love your stupid, arrogant ass." Letting out an exasperated breath, I spun on my heel to leave, but he quickly grabbed my wrist again.

"You love me Dedra?"

"Didn't I just say that… *stoopid*!" He chuckled at my response, and tugged me into him, releasing my wrist so he could rub on my ass through my lace boy shorts. My body reacted to his touch immediately, and I laced my hands around his neck.

"Daddy missed every inch of your sexy body." He kissed my stomach, his tongue playing with my navel, as he hooked his thumb in my underwear, slowly taking them off. I swear somewhere in the far distance I heard a choir singing *Hallelujah!*

Taking my left leg and hiking it up so that it sat on the edge of the bed, my right stayed planted on the floor; Dornell took his fingers and parted the lips of my pussy so that he could have proper access as he moved his mouth into me. At the first feel of his tongue on my clit, I tipped my head back and whimpered quietly, so as not to wake my kids. Digging my nails into his back to keep from falling from the intense pleasure I felt, I shut my eyes tightly, biting down painfully on my lower lip as Dornell expertly licked and sucked on my bud, pulling at it with his lips.

"This the best thing I ate all day," Dornell said in between licks. Let me just say this, my orgasm came so fast and so unexpected, it was damn near embarrassing. Dornell's mouth wasn't even on me a good two minutes, and I was already bussing all over his face.

"You got even better at that baby, I swear." I laughed as I reached down to unbuckle his jeans, his dick springing free as I took his boxers off. Placing my hand on his chest forcing him to lay back on the bed, I took my bra off so that I was completely naked and crawled up over his body, never taking my eyes off him.

Positioning myself over his rock hard dick, resting my hand on his chest, I looked at him and said, "This pussy..." I sat and eased him inside of me, licking my lips at the wonderful way he stretched me out, "belongs to you baby, and nobody else." His entire length now in, he placed his hand under my ass giving assistance that wasn't even required, as I bounced up and down on his dick. He grunted loudly, and I moaned out in raw lust as I finally was able to fuck the shit out of my man again!

That was three days ago; he's back with his family where he rightfully belongs. The bad news was Avion began feeling like a third wheel, and she left for good staying in her grandmother's cramped one bedroom apartment with her kids. I felt horrible when she told me she was happy for Dornell and I, but she decided to leave. I told her it was cool to stay, but she didn't want to.

"I got an interview tomorrow babe," Dornell said, bringing me back to the present. Dornell had been on a total of three interviews, and he still wasn't able to find a job. Our rent was due this month and between him and me, we were broke as a muthafuckin' joke.

"That's good baby," I replied, not sounding very enthusiastic as I packed the kids' lunches for school.

"Don't worry, I'll get a job soon, and we'll be back on our feet in no time." He walked over to me smiling, looking all handsome with his new haircut.

"Come on kids; hurry y'all lil' asses up or you gonna be late!" he yelled that out for like the third time since he was the one dropping them off to school. This time they finally came running out all smiles, happy to have their daddy home again.

"Don't even think about doing anything stupid Dedra. Don't get yourself involved in no stupid shit. Things will be just fine; give it some time." I looked at him a bit puzzled at first; exactly what the fuck did he mean by that? I knitted my eyebrows together as I looked up at him.

"I'm not trying to do what I did the last time Dornell; don't worry about it." He narrowed his eyes at me, something he did when he was giving me a final warning.

"Come on kids, tell your mummy bye." He eyeballed me again one last time. Ignoring his look, I walked him and the kids to the front door, saying my final goodbyes.

As if I wasn't just warned, like two seconds ago to be on my best behavior, I got my cell out and dialed up Gas' number.

"Speak," was all his ex-convict ass said as he answered the phone.

"Hey, it's Dedra; I just wanted to make sure you all ready for the next two days." I bit on my nails nervously, as I waited for him to reply.

"Yeah, we all set ma; don't worry your pretty little head." Wait, hold on a minute, did he just say we?

"What you mean 'we' Gas?"

"Oh, my homeboy about to roll with us." Aw, hell naw! This isn't what we discussed. Stormy would kill my ass if I told her about this shit.

"Gas, this is not what we planned. It was just supposed to be you remember, nobody else." I nervously began pacing back and forth in the apartment. See this was why Stormy said make sure I could trust him. And then his sneaky ass pulls some sneaky shit like this.

"Hey, a nigga like me can't be making these type of moves without a shooter by my side. Suppose some foul shit ends up popping off; who can I trust to have my back? You three bitches? Get the fuck outta here, I needs my man with me." I sat down at the edge of the sofa, my foot tapping as I listened attentively to what he was trying to explain.

It was most certainly too late in the game to get someone else, so I hoped and prayed this did not back fire on me.

"I hope its somebody you can trust Gas. I don't want any kind of bullshit, or it will be my ass! I need this to run as smooth as possible."

"I heard you ma, and I got you. You have nothing to worry about!"

CHAPTER EIGHTEEN

Chyna

Raging Bull

I swear on everything I did not mean for Trevelle to go flying down the flight of stairs the way he did. But it seemed as though ever since he met his father, he thought he could just mouth off to me if he felt like it. So as we were returning to this busted apartment Tremaine paid for for the next six months, I told Trevelle to stop slouching when he walks; his rude ass ignored me as if I were talking to that stupid PS4 game his dad got him, that he was busy playing with in his hands.

I told him again, and he flat out ignored me again! So you damn right I snatched his little ass up. He was a few steps ahead of me as we climbed the stairs, making our way to our floor. I grabbed him by the collar, but I must have grabbed at him a little too hard, when my hold on him slipped and he fell backwards, tumbling down a flight of stairs.

I thought he was dead at first, when I stood there looking at his lifeless body at the bottom of the staircase. I was scared to the point where I forgot how to even fucking move. When I called out his name, he stirred a little, and I raced to him.

So I called up his dad telling him he fell, coached Trevelle into saying he missed a step and tumbled all on his own, just in case his dad or the nosey doctors asked any questions. So here we are a few hours after, and I'm playing the part of a loving, concerned mother as I sat next to Trevelle's bed. While Tremaine is fussing over him like crazy, one would have sworn Trevelle broke his neck or something; all the fussing his dumb daddy was doing.

Hopefully this would be enough to make Tremaine invite us back over to his condo, because that flea infested apartment he got me and my son in just wasn't cutting it! Ok, so I'm lying…the apartment wasn't that bad; it was pretty nice and came fully furnished. But! I'm saying though, it's not like what Tremaine lived in. Why should Trevelle and I be subjected to staying in a regular, old apartment! I wanted to move on up like the Jeffersons.

"Hey, how you feeling lil' man?" I rolled my eyes so hard at the question Tremaine asked Trevelle, for like the fifth time as he stood next to his bed, hunched over, rubbing the top of Trevelle's head. Good thing his back was turned so he couldn't see my petty facial expressions.

"How'd you fall anyway again?" I immediately sat upright in my chair as I stared long and hard at Trevelle from over Tremaine's shoulder. Trevelle's eyes fell onto mine, looking a little petrified, as I mouthed the words…*I slipped and fell*, for him to repeat to his father.

"I just fell daddy," he said softly as he looked down at the cast that surrounded his broken arm; he turned his arm slowly taking a good look at it. I smiled and shook my head at his response just as Tremaine turned to look at me. The smile instantly vanished from off my face.

Tremaine rose up and walked towards me, hovering above me like some sort of dark cloud. I was actually a bit intimated to look him straight in his eyes.

"Get up!" he barked at me. Not even giving me a chance to reply, he bent and grabbed my upper arm roughly, literally dragging me from up out the chair I was sitting on. Pulling me out the door into the aisle, he took me to a quiet corner as he shoved his face a few inches away from mine. His face looking as if he was about to commit murder, but I had a set of lungs on me; when I started screaming this whole hospital would no doubt hear me.

"How the fuck did my son fall? Where the fuck was you Chyna? His arm broke in two different places; he's just three years old!" he boomed down at me angrily, his eyes piercing holes into mine. Fuck! I didn't do drama in school for nothing.

"Really Tremaine!" I yelled right back at him as I shoved hard at his chest; he didn't even budge. "You acting as if this shit happened on purpose! It was an accident. You think I don't feel at all bad that my son fell right before my very own eyes, and I couldn't stop it." Ok, I think maybe it's time for me to start with the fake tears.

It was as if someone turned a faucet on at the back of my eyeballs; those tears were running like a river. Somehow Tremaine didn't seem very impressed. "Here we go with those fake muthafuckin' tears again." He backed away from me a little, sucking his teeth loudly.

"I swear to you, Trevelle just tripped Tremaine," I said softly looking up at him, batting my fake eyelashes in the process. His expression didn't change, letting me know he wasn't buying what I was selling.

In a desperate attempt, I grabbed a hold of his face and crushed my lips to his, my hands snaking into his sweat pants smooth as butter, as I grabbed a hold of his nice, long, thick rod of correction and began rubbing on it vigorously as I shoved my tongue into his mouth.

Tremaine was obviously not impressed with my little PDA, and shoved me roughly away from him, slamming my back into the wall behind me hard enough that I got the wind knocked out of me a little.

Wiping his mouth with a look of disgust on his face, he pointed his finger in my face. "The next time you do that shit, I'mma bite your fucking tongue clean off. And when my son is released from out this hospital, he's coming to live with me. I've had just about enough of this cat and mouse game with you." Making those his final words, he spun on his heels and made his way back into our son's room.

I wasn't in the least worried about his silly little threat, because Tremaine, Trevelle and I would all soon be a happy family again.

Making my way to the restroom to check on my appearance, I re-touched my make-up and smoothed out my long 20" bundles and made my way back to my son's room. As I walked through the door, the image I saw caused me to freeze dead in my tracks.

Tremaine once again was hunched over Trevelle's bed, as Trevelle was whispering something in his ear. My presence went unnoticed for a couple of seconds before Trevelle's eyes connected with mine. Tremaine turned slowly behind him, and his eyes were bloodshot with rage, as he stood and charged in my direction.

I was scared out of my muthafuckin' mind; what did Trevelle say?!

Shit!

CHAPTER NINETEEN

Avion

The Plan

I left; those words replayed over and over in my mind as I sat in Dedra's car, along with Stormy. I left...that night at Tremaine's apartment when he had to go see about his son, I left even though he told me to wait till he got back. I still left. I don't know exactly why I did it, but I guess I felt as if I somehow didn't belong with Tremaine, like I didn't deserve him; Chyna and his son did...not me!

"Earth to Avion!" I jumped at the sound of Dedra practically screaming my name. I looked dazed as both she and Stormy were staring at me, sitting in the backseat of the car. So, guess where these two crazy bitches brought me? We were a few feet away from Richard's store, just sitting like a bunch of lurkers, watching everyone that came in and out.

"Sorry, I was thinking about something is all." Stormy rolled her eyes at me and turned her focus back to the store. She has been really getting on my nerves lately, but I wasn't one to lash out; so I kept it cool regardless.

"We don't have time for you to be zoning out into space Avi," Dedra chimed in. I rolled my eyes and looked out the window.

"So let me go over the plan with y'all." I sat upright in my seat as Stormy cleared her throat, and I focused on the entrance of the store.

"As I already told y'all, I can't go in when the both of you do, for the obvious reason that Richard will recognize me." I bent my head because I wasn't too happy about that part of the plan, but I did understand. Besides, Dedra and I were taking a risk ourselves. I mean Richard did see us that day when we met Stormy for the first time at the pharmacy. But Stormy said he was too focused on hoping that she didn't snitch on him to his wife, that there was no way he would he remember our faces.

"Now it will be closing time; the store will be empty except for the supervisor. She is going to be the one who will let you guys in. The supervisor...is with us! So don't worry that she sees you guys' faces. The inside guy got the supervisor on lock, she's not about to snitch; she wants to keep her job! So she's safe. Got that so far?" Dedra and I shook our head in agreement and Stormy continued.

"She's going to lead you guys to where the bathroom is. This is the part where you call me. I'll be in the getaway car with Dedra's guy. The supervisor will let me in, and I'll come meet you guys in the restroom. We'll mask up and make our way to Richard's office."

After those words were uttered, all three of us sat in silence as we stared at the store. I don't think any of us were even breathing.

Stormy continued, "The armored security vehicle will be there exactly twenty minutes after we get in there. We cannot afford to slip up! Richard would already have the money bagged out in his vault, waiting to be picked up. We make his ass lie on the motherfuckin' floor, take that shit and bust the fuck out of there."

"Richard is a businessman Stormy, and businessmen have registered weapons. What if he draws for his gun?" Dedra asked, as I placed my head in my hands. "Suppose he shot one of us?"

"I'll be right on him, and if push comes to shove..." The car went silent again, and I raised my head to the sight of both Stormy and Dedra staring at me in the back seat.

Why the hell they looking at me like that for?

"Wh---what? If push comes to shove what?" I asked, as I looked from Stormy then back to Dedra.

"We got us a shooter. Avion! We gon' need you to shoot that nigga.," I gasped in horror at what Stormy expected me to do.

"What! Stormy, we spoke about this. I don't wanna shoot anybody." My head was shaking from left to right like I was having some kind of panic attack.

"Man your weak ass up Avion! It's either that motherfucker, or one of us; and I choose him over one of us. If you need to whip your 9mm out and buss a cap in Richard's ass, so be it!" Stormy shouted at me, as I sat there in horror. Shit was fucking crazy, should have never met this bitch!

"Avion, we got this boo! You a sure shot; just aim for his shoulder, not his head or nothing," Dedra said as she tried to convince me. The palms of my hands began sweating like crazy; I was scared out my mind, but I still managed to shake my head slightly.

"Ok," I said softly as they both clapped their hands, as if what we were about to do was anything to celebrate.

"Now, your guy Gas, he needs to stay in that side street over there," Stormy said as she pointed to a narrow street not far from Richard's store. "It has to be that one, because the cameras don't work," she pointed to street cams that pointed to the street in question, "so we won't be seen. Richard has cameras in his store, but don't worry; my inside guy will adjust those so we won't be seen." My eyes grew wide, because whoever Stormy's inside guy was, dude was off the chain!

"So, when are we going to see who the fuck your inside man is Stormy?" Dedra asked twisting her neck, always with her attitude.

"After we do this and we're successful, he'll be revealed. You always pushy as hell Dedra…damn!"

"Shut the fuck up Stormy." *Oh, here they go again,* I thought, shaking my head as the two of them went at it, cussing each other out.

"Would you two chill the fuck out! You're like two children." They grew silent, and once again we all looked at the store, not saying a word.

"So ladies, tonight is our last night of being three broke bitches. I say we go hit a club…or two." Dedra looked from Stormy to myself, a big, broad smile on her face. And we smiled right back.

"Let's go party it up!" we all shouted in unison, as Dedra pulled the car out into traffic.

CHAPTER TWENTY

Stormy

Cousins Makes Dozens

If I get this voice recording one more time, I thought as I dialed Xavier's cell phone number. And just like the other five previous times I called, it took me straight to voicemail. I removed the phone from my ear and stared at the screen, as if it was my phone's fault he didn't pick up. I sucked my teeth loudly in anger because I hadn't spoken to Xavier all day, and I wanted him to swing by my apartment after I got home from the club.

Checking my reflection in the mirror, I knew my dress was way too short. I knew it was way too tight, and I knew it was cut way too low in the front, exposing my breasts... But I decided that this was what I wanted to wear. Tucking my phone into my clutch purse, I turned and headed down to the car to meet my girls, Dedra and Avion.

Xavier better had a damn good reason his phone was switched off. I walked towards the car and I opened the door, sitting down at the back.

"Bitch, fix your face." All I know was that Dedra better not start with me!

"Would you just drive and mind your damn business for once!" I didn't mean to shout, but I did anyway, and it was too late to take it back.

"Well damn! You sounding like I did when I wasn't getting any dick." She chuckled as she drove off.

"So, where the hell are we going anyway? All three of us broke as a joke. What club we finna get into?" Of course, I always knew somebody that could get us in his club for free.

"Just follow my directions, I know of a place," I said softly, as I gave her directions to one of the top clubs in Brooklyn. It's always good to keep niggas close enough...but not too close, for moments like this.

About an hour later we were in the VIP section of club Mo's, sipping on some expensive ass alcohol that none of us could even pronounce. Compliments of my friend that got us into the club for free.

We were all in a pensive mood, but we were still managing to enjoy ourselves. Dedra was wildin' out in her long, back-less white dress, with a slit that stopped midway up her thigh; she was trying her best to get Avion to twerk. But that was just a waste of her time, because Avion clearly had little to no rhythm.

I stayed more in the background, checking my phone every two minutes to see if Xavier called, but he hadn't, which was making me agitated as hell.

"Hey, I have to pee; let's all go." Dedra and Avion were standing beside me waiting for me to accompany them.

"Dedra, you already have Avion going with you, why I need to go?" I shook my head at her. I really wasn't up to walking anywhere, with anybody. Just wanted to stay my butt in one spot and get drunk!

"Oh my gosh Stormy, would you stop acting all salty; come walk with us, and maybe you'll see a fine nigga and forget all about Xavier dogging your ass." I cut my eyes at her and sucked my teeth, but decided to walk along with them anyways.

"Don't worry Stormy; I'm sure he has a good reason for his phone being off," Avion whispered in my ear, over the sound of the loud, blaring music as Chance the Rapper played in the background. I turned to her and gave a weak smile; Avion was actually starting to look a bit more at peace with herself. She smiled more, she seemed a bit more relaxed, she even looked as if she put on a few pounds, as I took in the way the short, baby blue romper she wore hugged her body.

We made our way to the restrooms and of course there was a long line we had to join in order to relieve ourselves. I could never understand why the lines to use the female restrooms were always long as fuck.

Finally, about ten minutes after, all three of us were making our way back to our VIP spot, when Avion suddenly grabbed a hold of both me and Dedra's wrist, causing us to stop and look at her.

"Hey, that's the woman." Confusion was now etched on our faces, because we had no clue what woman Avion was talking about.

"Avi, what woman? Are you drunk?" I heard Dedra ask her, as my eyes followed to where Avion was looking. But there were so many females standing around, I had no idea which one she was looking at.

"No I'm not drunk Dedra. That's the woman over there; the one I told you guys about when the kids went missing in the park, who was sitting beside me. There she go right there in the short, blue mini dress with that bright red lipstick on." So now Avion had me and Dedra's full attention; both of us were bobbing and weaving our heads as we tried to lay eyes on who Avion was talking about.

"I'll fuck that bitch up; where she at Avion?! All this champagne running through my veins, I'm about to get krunk and knock that bitch out!" We turned our attention to where Avion was pointing at, and it was like all three of us saw each other all at once! Mystery woman in blue laid eyes on both me and Dedra, the exact time we laid our eyes on her; her eyes landed on Avion first.

It was at that time she turned and bolted in the direction for the exit.

"Where does she think she's going? Hell naw!" Dedra said as she hit my arm and ran full speed in the direction that lady in blue went. Not putting any thought to it, I ran following Dedra out the exit of the club. But by the time we got out, that bitch was nowhere to be found; it was like she vanished into thin air.

"Shit! Yo that bitch lucky we didn't catch up with her sneaky ass." I put my hands on my chest as I tried to catch my breath. I needed to get my ass in the gym, I thought as I struggled to bring my heart rate down. I turned my attention on both Dedra and Avion, who were twisting their heads around in all directions to see if the lady could be spotted. But she was long gone.

"Come on y'all; let's go back inside. We'll see her again sometime,"

Avion said as she wrapped her dreads up since they came loose from our little sprint. Deciding we should just go on back inside and forget about that bitch, for now anyway, we made our way back to the entrance. When my eyes fell on somebody entering the club, somebody that I had to blink twice on seeing; because I knew my eyes must be deceiving me!

I guess both Dedra and Avion saw what I did, because the both of them came to an abrupt halt and turned to look back at me as I trailed behind them.

"Stormy, ain't that your man? Who the fuck is that bitch he's walking in with? Smiling and shit," Dedra said with a whole bunch of attitude as she stopped and pointed her finger at X. One would have sworn Xavier was her boo instead of mine.

Xavier didn't see us, as he was too busy leading this skanky ass bitch inside the club. I'm talking 'bout his hand resting on her lower back, guiding her into the club.

Pushing my way forward between Dedra and Avion, I made my way towards big headed Xavier.

"Aye!" I said as I used my palm to push against his arm, but he barely moved, even though I used a lot of force.

He turned to me and looked me over from head to toe. He was looking all kinds of delicious too. His cornrows were in a zig zagged hairstyle, his black, slim fit jeans hugged his sexy body, and his light blue polo shirt matched his blue Timberlands.

Not even showing any signs that he cared that I caught him red handed, he answered in a bland tone, "What up?"

This nigga right here…I was about to go the fuck off, and all he could say was 'what up!'

"Xavier!" I grabbed a hold of his arm and forced him to turn directly at me. "I've been calling your phone all goddamn day, and all you have to say is what up!" I shouted at him my hands were now all up in his face.

"Is this is why you've been unavailable? You out in these streets walking around with prostitutes!" I turned my nose up at the trick he was rolling with, her ass hanging all out the back of her shorts she wore, with a matching crop top showing off her pierced belly button. She was sporting a boy cut like Amber Rose, and she wore bright red lipstick on her full lips that brought out her caramel complexion.

"I suggest you train your pets before they come outside when they aren't domesticated Xavier." Oh hell no! I know she didn't just say that.

"Bitch! I will fuck your shit all the way up; don't come for my girl when we never sent for you." Dedra was at my side within a matter of seconds. Xavier just stood and glared at me, trying hard not to lose his cool.

"Aye, when you ready to come at me in a respectful manner Stormy, holla at a nigga. 'Cause you know I don't deal with no drama," Xavier said as he turned to leave with his little slut moving along with him. But I'd be damned if he was just going to walk in this club with another bitch while I'm standing right here!

"Oh, it's like that. Well the three of us about to party it up in this bitch together." I purposely squeezed my way in between him and this fake ass Amber Rose as I stood staring him down, my hands folded tightly against my chest.

"You so fucking childish Stormy, this my fucking cousin. I was in the club already...see," He said as he held his wrist out to me, showing the bright green wrist band. "I know the bouncer, and I came out to get her in with me. You don't even know how to ask a motherfuckin' question; always quick to act a fool in these streets. Move out my way," he said as he roughly pushed me to one side, making his way closer to the entrance.

"Baby, I got your purse you left in the car," a voice said as a guy came up to the girl giving her a purse, and bending to kiss her in the process.

Can you guys say embarrassed!

"Hi, I'm Denise, Xavier's cousin; and this is my man, Terrance," she said with obvious attitude as she rolled her eyes at me. Taking a hold of her man's hand, she marched angrily through the entrance, not even bothering to wait for me to apologize.

Turning to Xavier about to say a thousand sorrys, I was met with his palm up to my face.

"Save it Stormy, I don't even wanna hear it. My phone fell in water earlier today by the way; I'm going to replace it tomorrow. Move out my way; let me get back in this club and get drunk as fuck." Saying nothing further, I did what I was told so he could walk past me and get back in the club.

Feeling like a complete jackass, I stepped out the line and made my way over to where Avion and Dedra were standing, Dedra by the way had a stupid smirk on her face.

"Bitch! Oh my god, you almost caused me to beat your man's cousin ass," Dedra said as she held onto Avion's arm and doubled over, laughing her eyes out. And all I felt to do was kick her teeth down her throat. And then Avion started laughing also, both were looking at each other and ha-ha-ha-ing in my face.

"This shit is too funny; I can't wait to tell Dornell when I get home." Tears were streaming down Dedra's face as she laughed uncontrollably, and not being able to help myself, I giggled along with them.

"We going back in or na?" Dedra and I stopped laughing and turned our attention to Avion; she must be out her mind.

"Hell naw!" We answered at the same time, which caused us to start laughing again.

"Let's get the fuck up out of here; we have a big day ahead of us tomorrow anyway. Xavier will need to cool off before I step to him again." With our arms linked with each other's, looking like the three Musketeers, Dedra, Avion and I made our way to the car.

Because tomorrow is going to be a day we either end up dead, in jail or rolling in a bunch of motherfuckin' coins!

CHAPTER TWENTY-ONE

Avion

By Any Means Necessary!

I took my dreads and twisted them up into a tight bun to the top of my head, and exhaled loudly as I tried to calm my nerves. I felt like I was in some sort of dream, but I knew I wasn't; this shit was very much real. What Dedra, Stormy and I were about to do was very much real, and I for one didn't believe I was about to do what I was going to.

I stood in my grandmother's apartment, feeling my chest constricting from anxiety. Not so much for what was about to happen, but because this apartment was so fucking small! Like damn, how my grandmother even survived in this piece of shit apartment was beyond me. If all goes according to plan, I would buy her a nice house somewhere, so she could get out of this sweat box.

I laced up my low-cut, black Converse sneakers as I sat on the floor of the bathroom. I stood up and examined myself in the full length mirror that hung at the back of the bathroom door. I wore all black everything. A pair of black leggings, a plain black tee and absolutely no make-up on. With my dreads pulled up it would be a lot easier to place the mask over my face, when that time came.

The reflection that looked back at me seemed calm on the outside, but on the inside...my stomach had birds flying around in there; forget butterflies!

Grabbing the backpack that sat in the sink, I checked the few contents it held: my mask and a change of clothes just in case it was needed.

Picking the bag up, I opened the door to go sit and wait for the call from Dedra letting me know she came to get me. The plan was for Dedra to come get me, then we would drive over to Stormy's place and get in the cleaning vehicle that her inside man provided for us last minute, and make our way over to Richard's store.

As soon as I stepped out the door, my kids rushed up to me. "Are we going to the park tomorrow mummy?" they asked as they held on to my leg, looking up at me with hope in their big, bright, brown eyes. I smiled down at them, and bent to scoop my little one into my arms.

"Let's make a deal ok? You guys have until next week to tell me where you want to go for a nice long vacation, and I promise you, I'll take you guys there." If it was even possible, their eyes lit up even more, and they smiled at me broadly.

"Really mummy? Anywhere we want?" I smiled and touched my oldest on top of her head affectionately and shook my head yes. "Yes baby, anywhere you guys want." I knew I shouldn't be making promises I was not sure I could keep, but if everything went smooth and according to plan, I will take my babies anywhere their heart desired. I believe we deserved that much!

"Avi honey, did somebody die? Why you dressed like the grim reaper?" My grandmother came in the living room where I was now sitting with my kids, as they played games on my phone.

"No ma, don't be silly. I just wanted to wear black is all. Will you keep an eye on the kids for a couple of hours for me? Me and Dedra and Stormy have to run a couple errands, then I'll be back." I didn't really like lying to my grandmother, but let's be real; I couldn't really tell her the truth either.

"Ok, you know I love keeping an eye on my great-grand babies. But you be careful now, and hurry on back home; you know I don't like you out in the streets too much." I smiled lovingly at her. *I was definitely getting her that house,* I thought to myself just as my phone rang, and my kids handed the phone over to me. Dedra's name popped up on the screen.

Wasting no time, I swiped my finger across the screen and answered her call. "Hello," I said softly into the phone.

"Why in the fuck you whispering? Bring your ass downstairs so we could go get Stormy's crazy self." She hung up the phone, not even giving me a chance to reply. Taking my backpack from off the sofa, I turned to my kids, feeling my chest tighten as they smiled at me, not knowing what their momma was about to do.

"Come here and give mummy a big hug." Pouncing on top of me playfully, they wrapped they arms around my neck tightly, raining kisses on my cheeks.

"Bring pizza mummy, when you come back," Shyanne asked, as she wiped her nose.

Kissing the tip of her nose, I promised her I would bring a pepperoni pizza when I got back.

"I love you guys to the moon and back, you know that right?" They shook their heads vigorously as I got up and slowly walked to the front door.

Turning the knob slowly, I looked back at everyone one last time. They were now sitting on the couch with their grandmother looking at cartoons, oblivious to what I was about to do. But I was doing it for them, so that we could have a better life. I wanted to take my kids and get the hell out of here before Jamal came back a second time; because there was no telling just what he would do.

Making my way down the stairs to where Dedra was parked, I opened the front door, threw my bag in the back seat and sat down, closing the door behind me.

I felt Dedra's eyes on me and turned to look at her.

"What Dedra!" I said to her as she smiled slowly at me.

"You ready bitch?" she asked as I took in her black attire she wore that matched mine.

"As ready as I'll ever be. No turning back now bitch." She smiled and we high-fived each other, as she pulled out into the steady moving flow of traffic.

"Let's go get our *chargie* and do this!" Dedra shouted as we made our way to Stormy's place.

CHAPTER TWENTY-TWO

Dedra

By Any Means Necessary

"Ooh fuck!"

I put my hands over Dornell's mouth in an effort to quiet him, so our kids couldn't hear his loud ass. So here I am, in the next couple hours my life was about to change for better or for worse, and I was giving my man a quickie on our bathroom sink.

"Ssshhh! Dornell you're too damn loud, as usual," I said in his ear in a hushed tone as he continued grunting loudly. I swear Dornell couldn't handle pussy under these circumstances. I was butt naked, spread-eagled on the bathroom sink with Dornell in between my legs, pumping rapidly in and out of me.

"You love it baby?" I whispered into his ear, as I sucked greedily on his earlobe. He sucked in a loud intake of air, as he enjoyed the feel of my mouth on his skin.

"I fucking love this pussy." As if to prove his words, holding my inner thighs he spread me open even wider, so much that it actually caused me to be in pain, as he drilled in me even deeper. Now I was the one being too fucking noisy.

"Ah! Dornell, oh my god baby!" I hollered out as I bit into his shoulder, wrapping my arms tightly around his neck, because this was hurting too good!

"I'm about to buss, and I'm shooting everything right in you." Everything was going fine until he said that shit, because I knew I was ovulating and there was a ninety percent chance my ass could get pregnant; and I wasn't down with walking around looking like no damn elephant for the next nine months.

"Naw! Dornell, you better not cum inside me," I hollered as I started pushing against his chest. This dick was putting in that work alright; but I'd be damned if it gave me another baby.

He took my hands and pinned my wrists above my head, resting them against the bathroom mirror. I became a prisoner in his hands, not being able to move my arms.

"Shit, Dornell," I breathed breathlessly as he took hold of my lips and sucked on them hard, inflicting pain, his eyes never leaving mine as his dick slammed even harder into me. I whimpered in pain softly, but I held his gaze.

"I fucking love you Dedra. I want us to have another baby." I closed my eyes as he deepened the kiss, his tongue slowly caressing mine as he released inside of me, the warmth of his release trickling out of me a little.

We stayed like that for a few seconds longer, kissing each other passionately, me not even caring if he got my ass pregnant or not; the dick was that good y'all!

Ever had dick so good, you didn't care if that nigga gave your ass twins or not?!

Moving on…he helped me from off the sink as I turned to make my way to the shower, which was actually how all of this started in the first place. I was about to hop in the shower when his horny ass came in and jumped me. As I turned and made my way into the bathroom, he slapped my ass, causing me to scream out.

Dornell left me in the privacy of our bathroom so he could go check on the kids, and I hurriedly took a shower so that I could go meet up with Avion first, then we would make our way over to Stormy's place.

Wasting no time, I hopped out the shower making my way into the bedroom, running around like a chicken who had its head cut off. I grabbed up the pair of black leggings and plain black tee shirt, a look we all agreed we would wear. My low-cut, black Converse were already on my feet.

I was wiggling my fat ass into the leggings when the bedroom door suddenly opened and in walked Dornell, closing the door behind him as he leaned on it casually, staring at me, not saying anything.

"Where you in such a hurry to go Dedra?" he asked as he continued staring at me, his hands folded on his chest.

"Are you shitting me right now Dornell? I already told you I'm going to the mall with Avion and Stormy." I scrunched up my face at him in annoyance as he glared at me. *The fuck is his problem?* I thought to myself as I threw the tee over my head.

"Don't get yourself involved in no bullshit." With those words, he turned and left the bedroom, closing the door behind him. Dornell was bugging, but I didn't have time to deal with his mood swings.

Racing over to the closet and opening the door, I moved around a couple boxes to find the backpack that was hidden; the backpack that held the mask and a change of clothing. Throwing it over my shoulder, I made my way to the living room where the kids and Dornell were seated watching a movie.

I walked to my two precious angels and kissed each of them at the top of their heads, loving the way their hair smelled and felt. Knowing I could not get all emotional, I turned to Dornell and pecked him lightly on his cheek.

"Love you guys," I said softly as I made my way to the front door with my backpack in hand.

"Just remember what I said Dedra," Dornell shouted at me. I turned my nose up at him before closing the door, making my way down the stairs to my car.

Opening the door, I tossed the bag in the back seat and took my phone out as soon as I sat down, and dialed Gas.

"Oh," was all he said as he answered on the first ring.

"Oh my ass. Nigga you ready?" I asked as I placed my key in the ignition.

"I was born ready D." I rolled my eyes at his words. Taking a deep breath, I asked the next question, dreading the answer I would get.

"Is your friend still gonna roll with you?" I was praying he would say no, because lord knows I never told Stormy that Gas planned on bringing his friend along.

"Fo' sure he's riding with me." I cursed every cuss word I knew in my head, as I pulled the car out from my parking spot.

"Gas, I don't want any problems aight? Make sure your boy is good people." I shook my head knowing I should just go right ahead and tell him forget about his friend, but I didn't want to make any waves, so I let it rest.

"Don't worry about a thing D, you and your girls are in good hands." I don't know why, but somehow those words didn't sit too right with me. But I brushed it off and drove towards Avion's grandmother's house.

CHAPTER TWENTY-THREE

Stormy

By Any Means Necessary

"Mummy is doing this for you baby, so you could get better and grow up to be healthy." I kissed Racine over and over on her pink face, as she cooed at me. With tears welling in my eyes, I placed her back into her crib and stayed with her, caressing her face and her squirming feet as she drifted off to sleep peacefully. She was such a sweet baby; it hurt every bone in my body that Richard wanted nothing to do with her.

Shaking off the feeling of me feeling sorry for myself, I was already clothed in all black, low-cut Converse on my feet. Making my way to my bed, I got on all fours and reached for the backpack that was under the bed. My backpack, however, had a few more items than what Dedra and Avion's had. It had the mask of course, but I was the one that held onto the 9mm weapons that my friend back at the shooting range loaned me. He was so sprung off my ass, he didn't even bother asking me what they were for; and for that I was grateful.

Sitting on the bed with the bag on my lap, I unzipped it and inspected the contents. The guns were loaded and tucked safely inside of a secret compartment of the backpack; the mask and a change of clothing were also present.

Satisfied that all that was required was there, I zipped the bag and sat waiting on my phone call from either Avion or Dedra, letting me know they were downstairs. My mother was going to take care of Racine while I was gone.

My phone vibrated in my hand, and I exhaled through my lips softly before looking at the screen. When I saw the number I smiled; it was my inside guy.

"Hello," I answered, my tone barely audible.

"How's everything? You nervous?" I smiled into the phone, because believe it or not the last thing I was, was nervous; I just wanted to see the look on that motherfuckers face when he saw all his money walking out the door. Richard deserves every bit of what he was about to get.

"Nervous…no. Excited may be a better word." We both laughed like a couple of psychos into our cell phones.

"Good. I have faith in you and your girls. I know you guys can do this. You guys do y'all part and I promise you, I'll do my part." I listened attentively and shook my head in agreement.

"So, my first part is done. The cleaning van you guys need to pull up in front of the store in is parked downstairs at your apartment. The driver's door is unlocked, and the key is under the mat. When you guys get to store, don't worry about the van. I got somebody to move it while you guys are inside. Remember, the cameras in the store will be turned off, but they will only be turned off for exactly fifteen minutes; then they will be back on…automatically! So you guys need to be out of there by then." I was on my feet now, pacing the floor of my bedroom as I listened, biting my nails; because fifteen minutes is not a lot of time for three women who've never done this before.

"Ok, I got you…we'll make it quick."

"Remember, Richard has a gun in his desk drawer; whatever you do, don't let him reach in his desk drawer. If he gets his hand on that gun, he will not hesitate to use it." I bit into my lower lip, because I knew exactly what I had to do to make sure he doesn't reach in his drawer.

"Understood," I said confidently.

"Good, so you guys suit up and handle it! You and I both know that Richard deserves this shit; he got nobody to blame but himself." I smiled broadly. We said our goodbyes and hung up the phone.

I walked back over to my bed and sat down. Fifteen minutes is not much time, and let's face it, so much could go wrong in that short amount of time. It was up to me to make sure my girls didn't get hurt.

I looked at the three janitor jumpsuits folded neatly on the bed, just as the phone rang again. The all too familiar name and number flashed on the screen, and I answered.

"I don't dance now, I make money moves…these expensive, these is red bottoms…these is bloody shoes!" I swear Dedra was a fucking trip, but I loved her ass regardless.

"You ready bitch!" she shouted into the phone, sounding way too hyped if you asked me.

"I'm ready bitch!" I replied, grabbing up the backpack, stuffing the jumpsuits inside. I made my way across to my daughter's crib. Looking down at her, I smiled lovingly as I played with her soft, light brown curls. It was now or never; Racine's health depended on it.

"Well bring your scary ass downstairs then. Let's do this!"

Bending to kiss the top of my baby's head, I made my way to the front door, waved goodbye to my mother, who was sitting on my sofa, watching TV eating up all my damn food; and proceeded to Dedra's car parked out front.

"Dedra, you leaving your car here. We rolling in that over there," I said pointing to the company vehicle that belonged to the cleaning company we were pretending that we worked for.

Wasting no time, they climbed out the door and we stood next to each other, looking like a bunch of fucking triplets in our matching outfits.

"Let's go; the keys are hidden in the van." Opening the driver's door, I checked under the mat; and sure enough, the key was right where I was told it would be.

Dedra and Avion climbed in, and we all tossed our backpacks to the back of the van.

Putting the key in the ignition, I started the van and pulled out into the street that wasn't very busy. All three of us were silent as I drove off to Richard's store.

CHAPTER TWENTY-FOUR

Avion & Dedra

"Remember, head straight for the bathroom, throw the masks on, and come get me." I looked at Stormy as she spoke; we all were seated in the back of the van as we dressed in the janitor jumpsuits. Dedra nodded her head, and I did the same. My stomach felt uneasy as fuck; I felt as if I wanted to throw up.

"Avi, you good?" I looked up as I finished zipping the jump suit on. Of course I was nowhere near ok, but I had no time to chicken out now...it was a little too late for that. For some reason my mind ran on Tremaine, and I wondered what the fuck he would think of me, if he knew what I was about to do.

I felt like he was somewhere close by, watching us and shaking his head in disappointment. I shut my eyes tight in an attempt to shut out my negative thoughts.

"I'm good Stormy." I opened my eyes and looked at her, managing to give her a weak smile.

Focusing my attention off the fact that this jumpsuit fitted me like a fucking parachute, I looked over at Avion who looked like she was about to have an aneurysm, if you asked me. But she played it off well when Stormy asked her if she was good.

"She has no choice but to be good Stormy, she's our motherfuckin' shooter." I laughed, as I rubbed Avion on her shoulder, and she smiled at me.

"That's Gas over there Dedra?" Stormy asked, pointing in the narrow street right next to Richard's store; we were parked directly in front.

"Yeah, that's him," I replied hurriedly as I saw the passenger seat occupied with whomever Gas brought along with him. I said a silent prayer in my head, hoping by some miracle Stormy didn't see he had an acquaintance with him.

"Hol'up." Shit, God apparently didn't see fit to answer my prayers.

"Who the fuck is that with him Dedra? We agreed he's supposed to be on his own." So I'm looking over in the direction of the car, squinting my eyes like a goddamn fool; as if I don't know he has somebody else with him.

"Dedra, cut the bullshit! Who the fuck is that with him Dedra?" I bent my head looking at my Converse, thinking if I should tell the whole truth, or half the truth.

"I dunno Stormy! He said he needed to roll with his homeboy just in case shit popped off! That he couldn't rely on three females to have his back." The way that Stormy's facial expression changed, I swore she was suddenly possessed by some evil force.

"Are you fuckin' shitting me right now Dedra?! How long have you known about this? How do we even know we can trust his friend?" Stormy suddenly closed her eyes and rubbed on her temples as she spoke.

"A few days ago," I said softly, as Stormy's eyes flew open and stared at me in anger.

"I swear I ought to strangle your dumb ass!" She got up and actually lunged at me. Avion, on the other hand, was quick and held her back.

"Hey, hey chill out you guys. It's a little too late for us to do anything about Gas and his friend." I turned and cut my eyes to Dedra, 'cause really; how could she think not to tell either of us about what Gas did?

"If anything goes wrong because of this nigga Gas brought along, just remember it's on your fucking head!" Stormy said as she wagged her finger in Dedra's face, who was looking guilty as fuck. She could barely look Stormy in her eyes; she just kept staring at her Converse sneakers.

"Look, Stormy I'm sure everything would be fine." I was trying my best to lighten the mood, but really I was probably more skeptical than Stormy and Dedra combined. This nigga was somebody none of us knew, so we had no idea of his mindset.

Looking at the time on her watch, Stormy looked up at the both of us. "It's time."

I looked over at Dedra, she looked at me and took my hand and squeezed it, never taking her eyes off me.

"You guys look at me." Taking our eyes and focusing on Stormy,

Dedra and I still held each other's hand.

Taking our hands in hers, so all the three of us were now connected, she continued on, "The supervisor is expecting you. She'll open the doors and lead you to the bathroom. After that, you guys know what to do. The cameras are going to be off for exactly fifteen minutes from the time you enter the store. You all have to move as fast and as precise as you can. The armored truck is something we don't wanna clash with; those motherfuckers got guns bigger than us! When we leave, we get into Gas' car and dip." Dedra and I nodded our heads in unison, my palms sweaty as fuck.

"I'll bring the guns when I come in." She turned and looked at me as she said this, and I knew why she did.

"Aight ladies, let's do this!" Reaching over she slid the door open, and Dedra and I hopped out. We took the mop and buckets out, backpacks strapped on our backs as Stormy gave us a final head nod and slid the door closed.

Taking a deep breath, Avion and I made our way to the front door. Before we could even knock, the door opened for us. And a pretty chick with short red hair stood in front of the open doorway as she scanned us over quickly. If she was nervous we couldn't tell; her features on her face were pretty much normal.

"This way," was all she said as she led us in the direction I believed was the restrooms. Avion and I followed in silence, my head taking in the store that was completely empty. Looking at all the expensive name brand clothes, which were ridiculously priced, I just couldn't imagine why this loser couldn't even take care of his daughter!

"Cindy!" A loud voice suddenly boomed behind us, causing all three of us to stop dead in our tracks. Shit, I thought to myself, too scared out of my mind to even turn around.

"Yes, Mr. Villaruel," Cindy replied as she turned casually around, a small smile on her lips.

"Who the fuck are they?" I held my breath as I felt Avion grab my hand.

"Oh, the regular cleaners got called last minute to another store, so the company sent two replacements." Cindy could get a motherfuckin' award y'all; this bitch didn't stutter not one time.

Suddenly, it looked as if Avion was about to turn around. I squeezed her hand tightly and she slowly looked at me. With wide eyes, I shook my head no at her; because the last thing we needed was for Richard to see our faces before we had a chance to put our masks on.

Getting exactly what I was trying to say to her without any words, she turned her head and faced front.

"Aight, I'll be in my office then. Let me know when the money truck is here to collect." I heard his footsteps make his retreat, and I exhaled in relief.

"Sure thing, Mr. Villaruel," Cindy said as she started walking again, prompting us to follow her steps. Opening the door to what looked like the employee bathroom, she turned to us.

"Y'all bitches just lost about two minutes, hurry the fuck up." Saying nothing more, she turned and left us. Sprinting into action, we abandoned the mop and the buckets, and pulled the bags off our backs, resting them on the counter, unzipping them. We pulled our masks out, and Avion reached for her cell phone and dialed Stormy's number.

"Stormy, we're in. Do we have to come open the door for you?" I heard her say as I pulled the mask off, looking at it in disbelief, because it just hit me that I was about to rob somebody. Dornell would kill my ass!

Avion hung up the phone and looked at me. "She said she'll be here in a minute; Cindy's about to let her in." I swallowed loudly, making a gulping sound in the quiet bathroom.

"Take your mask out Avi," I told her as I paced the bathroom floor as we waited for Stormy to make her appearance.

"You nervous Dedra?" Avion whispered, asking me the obvious as she unzipped her backpack, taking her ghost face mask out.

"Of course I am, aren't you?" She shook her head and I stopped pacing, looking at her in astonishment.

"I just want this to be over with, and for none of us to get hurt is all." As I was about to answer, the door suddenly flung open, and Stormy walked in.

"Y'all bitches mask up; we got less than ten minutes left."

CHAPTER TWENTY-FIVE

Stormy

"Your girls are in; I'm unlocking for you." I ended Cindy's call. She called right after Avion did, and I climbed out the van, making my way to the store's front entrance. As I made my over, I looked in the direction of our parked getaway car and narrowed my eyes at two individuals who were looking at me from the rearview mirror. Where in the fuck did Dedra get this nigga Gas? I started itching just looking at him. I should have met with him first before I gave Dedra the OK.

It was definitely too late for that shit. I just had to hope and pray that Dedra made the right choice.

The door opened, and I walked into the store. Cindy nodded her head at me and we hastily made our way to the restroom. As we made our way, I looked at where I knew Richard's office was and couldn't help the smile that pulled at my lips.

Pushing the door open Avion and Dedra were standing waiting for me to show up.

"Y'all bitches mask up, we got less than ten minutes left," I said, as I closed the door behind us, with Cindy making her exit as she was no longer needed. Taking the backpack off, I pulled the mask out and slipped it over my head, Dedra and Avion following my actions.

We stood for a couple of seconds, staring at each other. Next, I reached in and took out our weapons and handed them one each. Tilting my head slightly, I nodded and turned, opening the door… leader of the pack.

Knowing Dedra and Avion were not far behind, gun in hand I slipped my free hand in my jumpsuit for a little device I believed I would need. It was a voice changer, because for obvious reasons Richard couldn't hear my actual voice.

Standing outside Richard's office door, I turned to Dedra and Avion, putting my finger to my lips, even though the three of us were quiet as fuck. I placed my ear up to the door and listened.

I heard Richard talking, and then I heard a woman's voice reply. With my hand on the knob, I looked behind me at Dedra and Avion one last time and pushed the door open, barging in as if I were the motherfuckin' police.

Raising the gun, I pointed it at him as he sat behind his desk. His wife was sitting on the opposite side of him. Oh this shit is about to be on!

The look on Richard's face when we walked in on him and his wife, his piercing blue eyes wide, his hands raised in the air with his punk ass. Placing the voice changing device to my lips, I spoke into it, "Nigga, you know what the fuck this is; get the fuck up!" My voice was sounding like something straight out of an alien movie. Hearing all the commotion behind her, his wife turned to face us and screamed out in fear.

Remembering the words of my inside guy, about Richard having a gun in his desk drawer, I saw his hand began lowering possibly to reach for his weapon. Putting absolutely no thought to it, I rushed up to his wife, holding her by her hair I dragged her up out of her seat. Holding her around her neck, I spoke into the device again, my gun never moving from its intended target.

"Get your motherfuckin' hands in the air, or I swear I'll split her head open with one shot." I stared at him, and it looked as if he was actually thinking about whether to put his hands up or not! Like, this nigga was willing to put his wife's life in jeopardy.

"Richard! Just do what they say," his wife screamed out at him, which seemed to snap some sense back into him. As he placed his hands in the air again, I thought, *what a loser*; I signaled for both Avion and Dedra to make their way to him as I kept his wife prisoner.

"Nigga, get the fuck up!" Dedra shouted at him, as she moved the gun to demonstrate her words with Avion right at her side, gun pointing at him also. Time was ticking, and this nigga was moving too goddamn slow.

"Nigga, hurry the fuck up and give us them motherfuckin' coins! Open up your safe." With Dedra's gun at his temple, Richard made his way over to where his safe was in his office and entered his code.

He slowly opened the door, and I smiled behind my mask at the three neatly stacked bags, which held his earnings for no doubt the entire month.

"Nigga, take those bags out and rest them at your feet," I yelled out to him. My hold tightened on his wife, who was whimpering like a wounded puppy.

Doing what he was told, he took the three bags out one-by-one, resting them at his black Steve Madden shoes. His hands still in the air, he turned and looked at me.

"You three bitches, think you'll get away with this? When I find out who the fuck you are, I'll gut the three of you one-by-one, with a smile on my face," he snarled, his upper lip curling as he looked at each one of us, before his gaze settled back to Dedra.

Taking a step closer to him, Dedra tilted her head, her ghost face mask looking intimidating as hell, as she turned the gun sideways, pointing directly at Richard's head. Feeling a bit uneasy, because in my head I was thinking she was a little too close to him, I began shifting uneasily from one foot to the next.

"Nigga…Fuck you!" she spat out at him.

And then everything unfolded as if in slow motion; Richard suddenly lunged for the gun she had pointed at him. Before I could even think to react, one single shot rang out in the quiet office. I heard Richard groan as he then screamed out in pain, as he fell with a loud thud to the floor.

The three of us stood in obvious shock as Richard writhed in pain on the ground, holding his shoulder, blood quickly soaking through his light blue shirt. Which one of us that actually fired the shot was unclear to me at the moment; all I knew was we had to get the fuck up out of here.

"Everybody grab a bag!" I shouted as I pushed his wife out the way, as she quickly crawled to her no good husband's assistance.

"Richard, Richard baby, are you ok?" Dedra, Avion and I raced to where the bags lay and grabbed them up one-by-one and ran out the office door as fast as we could.

"We can't leave anything behind, let's get our shit that we left in the restrooms," I shouted, as we maneuvered our way through the store.

Literally kicking the door open, we placed the bags on the countertop and slipped out of our jumpsuits and removed our masks. Dumping everything in the garbage under the sink, we stuffed our bag of money into our backpacks and headed out.

Racing out the entrance breathless as hell, my watch started beeping, letting me know our time was up.

"Fuck, we gotta move; the cameras will be back on." Avion and Dedra were trying their best to appear calm, but deep down, I knew they were probably fucking as terrified as I was.

Reaching Gas' car, we flung the door open of his Subaru, all three of us jumping into the back.

"Gas! Drive; let's get the fuck up out of here!" Dedra shouted at him as all three of us out of breath was looking all around, as if we expected somebody to appear out of nowhere and kill us.

Gas' friend, who sat in the front seat, slowly turned to us, and I immediately got creeped the hell out; the way he watched all three of us made my skin crawl. This nigga was grimey as fuck. His face was littered with tattoos; he had short dreads and a scar above his right eye.

"You remember the address I told you we driving to right?" Dedra said to Gas as he backed out the narrow street, his friend looking at me smiling before he finally decided to turn his scary looking ass around.

"Yeah I remember. Y'all ladies were successful with your lil' robbery and shit? Everything ran smooth?" Gas asked casually, as he backed out the street, just as I saw the armored security truck pull up at the front of Richard's store.

"Shit," I whispered as Gas pulled out, his foot heavy on the pedal as we peeled out down the street.

"Oh my god, I can't believe we pulled it off," Avion said, as she put her hands to her chest, breathing rapidly, her chest rising up and down.

"Oh my god, that shit was an adrenaline rush!" Dedra practically screamed, as she started laughing wildly. "I can't believe you had the balls to actually shoot him." I spun my head at what she just said.

"You can't believe who had the balls to shoot him?" I asked in confusion.

"You Stormy." Ok, so now I was really confused. I turned my attention to both Avion and Dedra.

"Wait, who shot Richard?" I asked, as they both were looking at me as if I had lost my mind.

"Stormy, you shot Richard," Avion said as she pointed at me, her eyebrows coming together as if she thought I was somehow losing my mind.

I shook my head in disbelief. "No, no I didn't. Avi…I thought that shot came from you." I pointed right back to her, as she and Dedra stared at me.

The three of us were so engrossed in our conversation, that we took our eyes off the road. Had we been paying attention, we would have noticed that Gas was no longer going in the direction that he was supposed to go. We would have noticed that he brought us to what looked like an abandoned warehouse. But we didn't notice, however, until it was too late. We didn't notice until the car was switched off, and Gas and his friend were now facing us in the back, with their guns pointed straight at us.

"All three of you shut the fuck up!" Gas' friend said as he grabbed Avion's bag from off her lap. Avion sat in the middle, Dedra sat on the seat behind Gas, and I was seated on the other end.

"Gas! What the fuck, what is this?" *As if they needed to read and spell for Dedra's stupid ass,* I thought as I shook my head in disbelief. I just knew I should have made sure on my own that this guy could be trusted.

Dedra went out and found the shadiest nigga she could find, and look where it got us.

"No hard feelings D, but a nigga got to do what a nigga got to do." Gas and his friend snickered like the two idiots they were.

"Oh my god! Please don't kill us, we have kids…please don't kill us." Avion sobbed softly, tears streaming down her face. And all I could think about was that I did all of this in vain, and I was going to die without my baby getting a second chance at life.

This shit was unbelievable. I felt my eyes well up with tears as Gas' friend reached and took my bag then Dedra's, from off our laps.

"Gas, please, please don't do this," Dedra whispered, as I felt a single tear roll slowly down my cheek.

"Don't worry, we'll make it painless.," Gas' friend said. As I felt the barrel of his gun on my forehead, I closed my eyes and awaited my fate.

POW! POW! Two shots rang out.

"Fuck!" The sound of Dedra's shout prompted me to open my eyes. I gasped at the sight of both Gas and his friend slumped over each other, a single bullet hole to their heads.

"Yo what the fuck," I whispered in shock.

Just then, I heard the sound of the car door being pulled open, a hand grabbed me and Dedra, and all three of us screamed out in fear. Three men, ski masks pulled down hiding their faces, dressed completely in black, just as we were, surrounded the car.

"Get out!" one of them demanded, as they dragged all three of us out Gas' car.

I was beginning to feel as if I were in some kind of motherfuckin' movie!

Gas and his friend were dead; three armed, masked gun men now had Avion, Dedra and I walking towards the abandoned building, as we were being held by our upper arms by each of them.

Looking at their hands, they each had our backpacks that held the money we stole from Richard. Avion started crying hysterically by the time we were led inside the building and was forced to sit on the cold, dusty floor.

"Avi, don't worry; everything will be fine," I said, as my voice cracked, knowing damn well I was telling a lie. I had no idea what was about to happen. I had no idea who these men were and exactly what they wanted.

"Aye, why don't you just take the fucking money and leave us the fuck alone!" Dedra shouted at the top of lungs, tears of fear running down her cheeks.

One of the masked men, gun in hand, hunched down on his legs so he was now at her level, putting his finger up to his masked face, he said to Dedra,

"Ssssshhhhh."

Standing up again, his gun pointed at us as we sat cowering together on the floor, the other two unzipped each bag, taking the bag of money out, one-by-one placing the bags on the floor in front of each of us.

The three of them now stood before us, just staring at us behind their masked faces, guns lowered at their sides as they each began looking at each other as if they were unsure of what they should do next.

Beginning to get angry and frustrated at the way things turned out, I opened my mouth to speak. "If you want the money, just fucking take it! And leave me and my girls alone!" I shouted feeling guilty; because of me, Dedra and Avion were probably about to lose their lives. I had no one to blame but myself.

The three of them stood there, refusing to say anything. Then finally, the guy that stood in the middle reached under his neck;

holding on to the end of the mask, he began pulling it off his face, as the three of us sat in disbelief that he was about to reveal himself.

Then we noticed the other two started doing the same, and were ripping the masks off their faces also.

Dedra, Avion and I gasped out loud at what we were seeing.

"Tremaine!"

"Dornell!"

"Xavier!"

All three of us sat in obvious astonishment as we stared into the cold, hard, angry faces of our men.

"What the fuck!" we all said together.

TO BE CONTINUED

FOLLOW ME ON FACEBOOK:

Amanda Rosales

Looking for a publishing home?

Royalty Publishing House, Where the Royals reside, is accepting submissions for writers in the urban fiction genre. If you're interested, submit the first 3-4 chapters with your synopsis to submissions@royaltypublishinghouse.com.

Check out our website for more information: www.royaltypublishinghouse.com.

Text ROYALTY to 42828 to join our mailing list!

To submit a manuscript for our review, email us at
submissions@royaltypublishinghouse.com

Text RPHCHRISTIAN to 22828 for our
CHRISTIAN ROMANCE novels!

Text RPHROMANCE to 22828 for our
INTERRACIAL ROMANCE novels!

Get LiT!

Download the LiTeReader app today and enjoy exclusive content, free books, and more

Do You Like CELEBRITY GOSSIP?

Check Out QUEEN DYNASTY!
Visit Our Site: www.thequeendynasty.com

CPSIA information can be obtained
at www.ICGtesting.com
Printed in the USA
LVOW10s1632261017
553884LV00015B/890/P